THE
BEFORE-
LAND

THE BEFORE-LAND

A NOVEL

CORINNA VALLIANATOS

ACRE

CINCINNATI 2020

Acre Books is made possible by the support of the Robert and Adele Schiff Foundation and the Department of English at the University of Cincinnati.

ISBN-13 (pbk) 978-1-946724-38-0
ISBN-13 (ebook) 978-1-946724-39-7

Designed by Barbara Neely Bourgoyne
Cover art: Unsplash. Photo by Camille Villanueva.

This is a work of fiction. Names, characters, businesses, places, events, and incidents are either products of the author's imagination or used in a fictitious manner. Any resemblance to actual persons, living or dead, or actual events is purely coincidental.

The press is based at the University of Cincinnati, Department of English and Comparative Literature, McMicken Hall, Room 248, PO Box 210069, Cincinnati, OH, 45221–0069.

Acre Books books may be purchased at a discount for educational use. For information please email business@acre-books.com.

For H & D

THE
BEFORE-
LAND

THE BOY

They pulled out of the gas station. His grandmother's profile stern in the golden light, her sinewy foot in its Birkenstock sandal pressing the accelerator. The boy thrilled to how fast she drove. They were headed south, and it made sense. All things sank eventually. To an out-of-the-way place, if *way* was where other people were. He unrolled his window, and the bleating highway air rushed inside, filled his shirt, flapped its collar. They weren't on the coastal highway, the pretty one. They could no longer see the Pacific. But it was there, somewhere off to his right. In Eureka it had been a constant presence, sopping the harbor, filling the bay, staining the sand and sky. Now he sensed it more than felt it, a tumbling of soft teeth. They drove for hours before they neared Los Angeles. There they turned east, past lines of little stores like candy dots on paper: key cutter, nail salon, outdoor furniture, plaster statues. Car dealership whose long windows reflected the mountains. His grandmother had told him not to drink anything so they wouldn't have to stop. I've got a lot to teach you, she'd said, now that we're on our own. Which confused him, because it had been just the two of them for as long as he could remember. He supposed she meant beyond the grip or view of anyone else. A feeling she'd always exaggerated, that someone was watching. They were on Foothill Boulevard, the old Route 66. Palms with heads like flattened nests. Drive-through fast food, loose-jointed lines of cars. Finally they turned and drove down a different road, and turned again and traveled quietly through a small town bristling with trees, a place that seemed stilled, crouched against what they'd just passed as if against blows from a fist, but they didn't stop there, they kept going, the road narrowing and rising gently into the mountains, winding as it rose, cacti, agave, the sun tangled and pressing down on them.

ONE

STONE JAY

There were no houses this far into the canyon, nothing but a boy wading a thin river and an old woman sitting with her feet plunged into a Styrofoam cooler, watching Stone Jay's approach.

"Not much going on here, is there?" he said to her. "Pretty empty, isn't it?"

The old woman replied that the canyon's emptiness was exactly what was so agreeable about it, and he said she was right about that. The sun was like a hand throwing dice that scattered, the rays fell far apart. She withdrew her feet and a couple of tins of sardines from the cooler.

"Are you gonna stare, or are you gonna have some?" she asked.

The boy joined them in wet tennis shoes and a long lavender dress shirt whose tail was soaked through. As they ate, the old woman reminisced about her childhood. She said she'd had to call her father—the boy's great-grandfather—Your Honor, and he'd teased her mercilessly and told her she had chicken-skin arms and a weak constitution, and her mother had done nothing to stop him. The boy lifted his head from its sardine-and-cracker-wolfing hunch, and Stone Jay saw a quivering attentiveness in his face, a pure appetite.

"What did you do?" he asked.

"I was too young to know otherwise. That ignorance. That's the way they get you."

She drank from a plastic jug of water, then passed it to Stone Jay. "Hiking through or staying put?"

He looked down at himself in his jeans and ripped Vans and socks pink from the wash. "Neither, really. I didn't expect to be here."

"Expect? What, do you lie around expecting things? Expecting, waiting, wishing, wanting, whiling away the hours? I didn't anticipate being here; it wasn't in my *datebook*. Well, you are! So what are you going to do about it?"

He drank greedily until she flapped her hand for the jug's return.

"I'll be on my way soon."

She snorted.

"I'm not setting up camp, I'll tell you that," he said, nodding at the tent pitched nearby.

"No, it seems not," she said.

"What about you?"

"We're chasing the sun."

"Where're you from?"

"Northern California."

"It's different down here. Do you miss it?"

She turned to the boy. "Do you?"

"Miss what?" the boy said.

"He wants you to say something about the place where you lived, to share your thoughts."

The boy shrugged.

"He keeps his thoughts to himself," she said.

It was late August. A few spindly trees grew right out of the river, their roots half exposed, humped and clutching, like talons holding scraps of water. Why this landscape, this crack in the San Gabriel Mountains, should be considered superior to the things of people—stucco stores and houses, strip malls and boxy office complexes with their second-floor breezeways, their black railings like stained teeth—Stone Jay did not understand. The mountains had history on their side, but history was heavy, paralyzing. No, give him the electronic bleat of a convenience-store bell, the cold, marbled air inside a row of refrigerators . . . give him the indoors, where he knew what was what, how to walk into a room, how to walk out again. Where history was constantly replaced. But here he was, because after a friend had invited him to crash at his parents' house, Stone Jay had wanted so badly to have something to counteract his sister's disapproval, somewhere to flee from her dismay (though he was the cause of it, wasn't that always the case?) that he'd allowed her to drop him off in the middle of nowhere. He rested his elbows on his knees and turned his face from the sun. Even sitting still he had the sensation of fleeing, sinking-ship skip in his chest, sweaty bandana he wore around his forehead slipped down to encircle his neck. He heard the old woman get up.

"Ready?" she said.

"Let him come too," the boy said. "It's always me and you."

"Your point is?"

"I'm bored of it."

"A person with a brain can't be bored. The two things are diametrically distinct."

Stone Jay raised his head. "Excuse me," he said. He approached her where she stood riffling around in a canvas knapsack. "Forget him. I'll get you out of here."

Her hand stilled. She spoke past him to the boy. "How do you like that?" She withdrew a snub black gun stippled like fake leather, and pointed it at him, her wrist wobbling. "The male can't tell when he's not wanted. The male's blindness is dangerous. Not you, you know better, and maybe not this one in particular, but I don't care to take any—"

The boy stepped forward, and she allowed him to remove the gun from her hand, and he shot her in the hip. She cried out, by the sound of it more aggravated than hurt. The boy dropped the gun, and she kicked it away scornfully and sat down.

"What did you do that for?" she said. She flopped onto her back. "It's not a *stick*. It's serious. . . ." The boy dug into her pockets, first one and then the other, which was darkening with blood, and pulled out a set of car keys.

"I'm taking these," he said.

She did not reply. He grasped her ankles and nodded that Stone Jay should take her under her arms, and they carried her into the tent.

Smell of nylon and beach-umbrella light. The old woman's head lolled, her long throat with its ruffles of fat pulled tight. They lowered her to the ground. Stone Jay unknotted the bandana from around his neck and refolded it so the fresh side was facing out. He pressed it to her hip, against the fluted curve of bone.

"I didn't think it was loaded. I never saw her load it once," the boy said.

What he was touching seemed incredibly intricate, like the edge of a champagne glass. Her chest rose and fell. He pressed harder, and it rose and fell more quickly. He positioned the bandana beneath the waistband of her slacks and took his hand away. To observe someone's pain and not feel the pain yourself was the only reason anyone could walk around doing the things they did, he thought. He felt something, but it wasn't pain. There was a tarp in the corner. The boy shook it out, filling the tent with its crackling, and covered the old woman with it, tucking it in at her sides.

"Are you awake? Doreen?" The boy slapped her lightly and turned to Stone Jay. "She's not awake."

"You stupid kid," Stone Jay said.

The boy ducked outside and he followed, watched him track the shallow furrow of the gun's path to where it had come to rest—spun away from the tent, cockeyed and glinting—and lift it with forefinger and thumb and plunk it into the old woman's knapsack. He watched the boy draw the bag's cords tight, sling it over his shoulders and scramble up an incline of loose dirt and pebbles that sprayed against Stone Jay's ankles. This higher land was hotter and drier and littered with chaparral, the tufted green tops like stiffly arranged bouquets that in outlasting their beauty had grown more definitive. Eucalyptus trees wept long sashes of bark spotted with wavy eyeholes. The boy walked purposefully, and Stone Jay, who kept pausing, wavering, half-turning back, had to hurry to keep up with him. Eventually they came to a car parked behind a cluster of the cream-skinned trunks. The boy hiccupped toward the driver's-side door, then went around. Inside, it smelled of heat and grease and fruit punch.

"We need to go back for her," Stone Jay said, and the boy could tell, Stone Jay knew, that he didn't mean it, and the way the boy did that, slivered into him, made him furious.

"She won't come. Not with you." The boy reached across the seat and fitted a key into the ignition.

"Alone, then. Just her grandson."

"I barely nicked her. You don't know her. She won't want to come with me either."

"We can't leave her."

"That's all she ever wanted," the boy said, "to be left. To be just like this."

Stone Jay gripped the steering wheel and felt a collapse inside him, a deep fold of recognition. The seats were crosshatched with electrical tape, the glove box held shut with it. The car had seen better times, but it waited here heavy as a safe. His problems had grown from what to do now to what he should've done before this, impossible to fix because the past was a dark and swimming thing, drifting forward even as he thought of it.

Someone's studio, someone's storage unit, someone's garage. Anything would do, but an empty house his sister, a realtor, was selling would do even better. This was a squatter's paradise, these ceiling fans and carpeted floors, venetian blinds and working plumbing. When Stone Jay invited his sister's husband over he never expected that Wilson would accept. He played it cool, offered his vape pen, suggested they rise at the break of dawn to get breakfast. He thought the break of dawn was a nice way of putting it, but Wilson said he'd be home before then.

Wilson vaped with a graceful wrist and a deep, attractive squint. If you want to sell your house, you have to put away your refrigerator magnets and dog beds, Wilson said. Apparently refrigerator magnets and dog beds are huge turnoffs. Your sister taught me that.

Oh yeah? he said.

Yeah, Wilson said. They're too human or something.

Yeah? he said. What's human about dog beds?

The way they're all scattered *around*, Wilson said.

Stone Jay pissed into the gas fireplace while Wilson laughed in the background. It was all background, that was what happened, rustling fields of wheat and a diffident happiness he was fearful of ending, for it would end with him being low and sure again. He wanted the wheat to go on rustling, the feathered heads to slap and shiver, this wave of growing warmth to wash and wash over him.

Can I kiss you? he said, and did so without waiting. Sorry. Sorry, sorry, I meant it to be friendly. I never do anything right. I mean, I'd be open to you if you were open to me in a natural way, like being humanly connected, *man* the connections that humans can make, but but but *but* I don't want to diminish the fact that you may not have expected or wanted that, so my apologies, my apologies. I duff my hat, I prostate—

Prostrate, Wilson said.

Prostate myself before—

Shh, Wilson said. Let's sleep.

An old man's reaction if ever there was one, though maybe he guessed how early Stone Jay's sister was bound to appear, and indeed she showed up first thing next morning and started right in with the house had been sold or was going to be soon or never would be with him hanging around—he knew what she was building to and he didn't want her to get there, so he flung himself in front of his ejection, said this prep cook he knew (called Aaron Mayonnaise) had a place in Palmer Canyon (or his folks or something did), and all he needed was a ride. All he needed ever again. And though it did not come naturally, Please, he added. She stilled for a moment, and he knew she was asking herself the only question about him she'd ever asked herself, which was where he would be less trouble.

Okay, she finally said.

Wilson climbed into the backseat, and they drove out of town. The road narrowed and the air grew cooler and the foothills reared up around them like a huge dry animal caught in a net. Sun-shot leaf shapes flew over the windshield and the engine strained and he felt his ears pop and the tires moved from asphalt to dirt until there was nowhere left to go except a fire access road.

Really? his sister said. You really mean *here*?

WILSON

He forced himself not to look back as she pulled away. "You okay?" he asked, leaning forward and putting his hand on her shoulder. Audrey was navigating her way out of the canyon, and apparently it took all her concentration. She lifted her shoulder just slightly, whether in answer to his question or to shrug him off he couldn't tell. He removed his hand, wondering again why it had seemed like a good idea to join Stone Jay at Bonita Street. Well, it had never seemed like a *good* good idea, but he'd wanted a smoke, whatever Stone Jay had, even just a cigarette. After the quinoa and chickpea salad she'd made for dinner, he'd wanted it badly. He had cravings. Salty crackers with port wine cheese, French fries, beer. So he'd stopped by and—

"Shit." The car swerved. "Coyote," Audrey said.

—and yes, smoked his pen, splayed out on Stone Jay's sleeping bag, listening to him going on and on about whatever he was going on about, his words like background music to background music, and when Stone Jay lay down beside him and began to touch his face he assumed his ministrations were medical, that he was bleeding or something, and then Stone Jay's hand was on his chest as if he were saluting the flag, sort of at an angle, and Wilson felt himself drifting, observing his own body with a very mild, gauzy interest rather than the laser eyes of disapproval Audrey always turned on him, and it felt good, both the release of scrutiny and the physical sensation of Stone Jay's lips, which were dry and scraping, inexact and strangely pleasant.

"Which is meant to be out here, which has fur. As opposed to a human with its—"

"Skin," he supplied.

"I know that. I mean its lack of instinct. I didn't see any friend or anything there."

They came down out of the canyon and took Indian Hill south, all the pretty houses singing past, all the red tile roofs and fig trees and lush sprinkler-fed lawns. "I've humored him and humored him, and I can't do it anymore," she said.

"No, you can't," he said.

"He's my younger brother. I didn't want it to be like this."

"Of course you didn't."

"His whole life he's been running away from himself."

"Or being chased."

"Stop *agreeing* with me," Audrey said.

They drove through downtown, past the stores just opening their doors, the boba teahouse and mini-pie place and the skateboarding shop with the very lovely salesgirls, he'd heard, though he had no occasion to frequent a skate shop and would not, as some of his colleagues had done, take up longboarding in his fifties. Dentist's office that offered environmentally friendly fillings, home furnishings store that sold canning-jars-turned-light-fixtures and koi-shaped oven mitts. They crossed the train tracks and entered a modest neighborhood of ranches with RV-wide driveways and leggy bougainvillea splayed over gates and walls. Cacti grew from raked white gravel yards. His stomach did a complicated clench and release as they pulled up in front of the house on Bonita. There was a black lockbox on the doorknob, from which Audrey retrieved a key.

Inside, they followed the smell of pot and piss and Pine Sol to the den. Empties everywhere, and a metal pen and two prescription bottles of Clorazepate and Prednisone made out to a canine named Homer. Wadded checked shirt, *Parade* magazine open to a recipe for watermelon soup, library book receipts with names and phone numbers written on them. There was something about the foolish hope invested in Kerri at 909-370-1959 that tugged at his heart.

"I've seen worse," Audrey said.

"It's not fair," he said. "Why should you have to clean up after him every time?"

"Why, why, why? It's such a self-defeating question."

She crossed in front of him on her way to the hallway. She was tall and thin, with a spine like an iron rod and shiny black middle-parted hair that she tucked behind her unpierced ears. As her steps clicked away, some spike of indignation that had organized his emotions gave way inside him. He lowered himself with a groan to the sleeping bag. He was fifty-four, too old for this. There was a river of time that he rowed against at Monroe College, his students younger and younger each year, aging him doubly as he aged. Something hard dug into his back. When he fished it out of the sleeping bag he saw it was his phone. His phone, Jesus. He hadn't realized it was gone. There were two messages.

The first was from the chair of his department. "Wilson, this is Cora. I wanted you to be one of the first to know that we made an offer, but you're actually one of the last. Blame the Byzantine channels of communication around here. Blame me. I know you must be angry, and I appreciate why, I do, but try, too, to appreciate our position, how much we needed someone who's . . . it sounds vulgar to say, but, well . . . publishing. If you'd have just—and believe me, I understand how invested in your book you are, how deeply you've tunneled into it, and of course you can't rush a thing like that because it would feel rushed, and just as a side note, I stand behind it unwaveringly, I think it's an incredibly important project, but in the meantime the department's needs were going, I don't want to say unmet, but somewhat less fulfilled, less robustly actualized than we'd hoped for. Hope. What a fickle thing. Don't think I'm unaware of how long you've been teaching for us, or how you'd hoped—there that word is again—that this new line would go to you, as you should have seniority on your side. . . . " She paused, and her voice crumpled into a softer, lower register. "If it were up to me things would've gone differently. Come to my office, and we'll talk about your new schedule."

He pressed delete. He could easily enough discuss his new schedule with her via email. What she really wanted to do was get him alone and smash him with her sympathy, steamroller him with her understanding. "If things were up to me you'd only be teaching workshops," she'd said the last time he was in her office, gazing at him with her tapioca-colored eyes. "Because your students adore you. Obviously. You married one."

Ouch, he was supposed to say, clutching himself beneath the rib cage. *You got me.* Though actually, Audrey didn't adore him; she didn't even act as though she liked him very much. He'd given her a B (really, she deserved a B-), and she'd gone on the warpath to get it changed to an A. Which he didn't do. She was a fairly poisonous presence in class, a skeptic, a naysayer, a cataloger of what was wrong with a piece, never what was right, and she wasn't at all liked by her peers. He'd see her standing alone during break, casting sidelong glances at the crowd as if she wanted to belong, but then, when class started up again, her comments would be even more biting than before. When he told her he wasn't budging on her grade he could sense that she'd known he wouldn't, that the fight mattered to her more than the outcome. She'd said not only was all art subjective, an assessment of someone else's facility in creating and/or talking about art was too, which meant the grade he'd given her was a projection of his own prejudices and should be subject to discussion and change. She said the kind of person who gave a lot of Bs was a timid person, a person who wanted it both ways. What makes you think I gave a lot of Bs? What makes you think yours wasn't the only one? he asked, and told her to go to the chair—he forgot who it was then, not Cora—with further concerns, and she left his office in a huff, and he didn't give her much thought until a year later, when she had *already graduated*, and she showed up during his office hours

16

and asked him out for coffee. He'd thought about how she'd been so roundly rejected by her classmates before he said yes. That thought definitely occurred to him.

But instead of saying this or any version of this to Cora, he had simply laughed. He refused to react to her jabs, so she wouldn't have the pleasure of forgiving him.

And he had a secret. There was something Cora didn't know, and it was, he thought, the most crucial fact of all. He wasn't writing anymore. He wasn't wrestling with any book of poems about a hawk that fought alongside the Massachusetts Infantry's Fifth Regiment during the Civil War, though he'd certainly let it be known that he was, talking about it at department meetings with increasing avidity and the fond frustration he supposed a writer in the thick of a project might feel. But it was all fake, the groaning and sheepish admissions of progress, giddy, halting, glorious progress. When asked about the book at the last meeting, he'd actually said, The end may be near! and his voice had caught, and a few people had turned away with the swift fright of those who don't want to witness a grown man cry.

He hadn't been. His throat had constricted with humiliation.

If he'd trained to be a medic, a librarian, a lawyer, he'd have something now, the beauty and, he'd daresay, the poetry, of vocation. One line of it after another: getting up, getting dressed, making minor movements that in general helped others . . .

Instead he taught undergraduates how to make their poems about their Caribbean vacations better. The *detail* that dramatizes the gross disparity of wealth, that's what we're looking for, detail not declaration. . . .

He sighed and played the second message. It was Stone Jay, giving him the address of the house where Wilson lay right now.

He walked down Bonita to College. It was the first day of classes, and students swarmed past him. It seemed no one could be ugly anymore, it seemed there'd been a generational genocide against ugliness and the new regime had decreed only clean gliding limbs and pre-ripped denim were allowed. The sun stroked down. He remembered how he used to live in jeans, how the fabric would pale and loosen, soften into silk, and he'd know a rip was coming before it came, the mouth opening over his knee.

He reached his office and ducked inside. The phone light blinked arrhythmically, a twitching red eye. He stood in front of the shelves and studied his books of poetry, the way they leaned and slipped against each other, the way they buckled and heaved as if weak with laughter. They were like people who'd just heard something unflattering about one of their own, something that immediately rang true, and were trying, failing not to lose it as the one of their own stood among them, unknowing, naïvely believing he belonged.

Snobs! he thought, and swept them, shelf by shelf, to the ground.

They fell in hard wet splats, like magazines. There was a moment of silence, and then a knock on the wall connecting his office to his neighbor's, and Midge DeWitt, Milton scholar, Midge of the cork-soled sandals and bent toes and a certain fuck-you-ness in her thunderously frizzy hair, Midge of the clamorous turquoise jewelry and catastrophic shits (as he'd discovered once, using the restroom after her and witnessing the lacy scraps and grass clippings she'd left behind), Midge of the private trudge toward lonely oldness that seemed still more obvious against the heartiness of her voice, Midge called out, "Wilson! Did a little earthquake strike in there?"

"Sorry for the racket," he called back and slumped to the floor, surrounded by his Yusef Komunyakaa and Philip Levine, his Dean Young and Robert Lowell. (He needed to read more women.) Doors opened and closed, and his colleagues came and went, greeting each other in code, "Here we go again!" meaning *We have students in common and I hear your classes could use a spanking into shape*, and "All well at the writing center?" meaning *You're like a car mechanic who works on sentences*, and "Eva happy at Wesleyan?" meaning *How many tutors and virtuous summer camps did it take to get her in?*

Or was he the only one who thought such things? Who took the banal and made it ugly? It was impossible to ask, it was the loneliest thought in the world. . . .

Yet thoughts like that had led him to poetry, which was where, he'd supposed, he'd untangle them and find their truths. He opened *Life Studies*. The table of contents was a long black comb with uneven teeth. The pages crackled comfortingly. Lowell had New England on his side. Wilson was from Arizona, where restaurants misted their patrons like grocery store vegetables. At best his pain was ordinary, at worst his pain was ordinary. But the hawk was extraordinary. The hawk was brave and loyal to its men, ranging free yet always coming back to them, even when the regiment had moved on. It always found them. When it was grazed by a bullet during a skirmish in Pennsylvania, the soldiers decided to install it in a hotel, where it would be comfortable and safe and they could take turns visiting it. And they did, one by one, stroking its head and unburdening themselves of their sorrows, their fears. The hawk groomed their eyebrows, and they fell asleep next to it and dreamed of home. But the ending was not happy. There was a fire. This would be the final poem, the death of the hawk. He could see it, perched on a velvet settee. A smattering of fruit on a crystal plate. Smoke snaking under the door to its room.

In camp with its men, it could out-fly death, climb through the air to the startled tops of trees. In the hotel, it could only throw itself against the window again and again.

Its doomed battering. The glass panes smeared with oil from its feathers and nicked by the blows from its beak.

The hawk was trapped inside him. Sometimes he felt its flexing, its powerful preening and animal optimism, and then he thought that he would write it back into the world. But most of the time it was fast asleep, and he knew it would stay that way.

The truth had made him into a liar, so what was so good about the truth?

Long ago, when he was a just a little older than his students were now, he'd thought he had to write about rocky promontories. Or the verge of a lake, or factories. He thought that was the choice—you were either a poet of rocky promontories or factories. So much of him existed in the gap between the real and the imagined, the dull actual course of events and the blazing other path. Not his soul exactly—a vague word—but the tar of him, the building cells. When he met friends for drinks, he tried to steer the conversation toward this phenomenon, that which was eluding them all. They should've been feasting on sweets, kings at a buffet. They should've been living among horizons. Instead they were lonely, peevish, paranoid. He remembered one of his friends saying that he'd gone to a party dressed like a lizard, but when he got there he realized it wasn't a lizard party, it was a wizard party, and Wilson remembered saying, Well, couldn't that be good? If the theory of opposites attract holds at all? and the silence that followed indicated that it did not hold. That lizards and wizards weren't opposites, and he'd missed the point again. And again he'd had the feeling of clouding whatever room he walked into, messing with its easy vibe, dampening the gathering just slightly. Sometimes he felt so extraneous, so absolutely inessential, that he left the table for the sanctuary of the men's room, entered a stall and sat down. It was an immersive and quotidian fear. It was the fear of being a drag.

STONE JAY

The car was stick, so they switched places. The boy took off his shoes. He liked to feel the pedals, he said, scooting forward on the seat. His grandmother had taught him to drive because she expected a day like this to come. She was always planning for the worst. He took Palmer Canyon Road too fast. "Slow down, slow down," Stone Jay said, and the boy jerked into a lower gear. They came stuttering out of the canyon and went east on the I-10, past brown rows of houses that led like flagstones to the feet of the mountains, past the rainbow bands of light that played up and down over a jumbo electronic sign advertising a mall and movie theater with recliner seats. After a while, the boomerang-shaped hotels of the Morongo Indian Reservation's casino became visible, early September, REO Speedwagon there for a three-night gig. Long lines of white wind turbines spread out over the San Jacintos. On the ridges they looked like white porcupine quills, and then, as the car got closer, like slim bleached trees, and when the boy turned off the 10 onto Twentynine Palms Highway, they drove through a kind of undulating field of the hulking, graceful things, with blinking red eyes like a faithful dog's.

The turbines gave way to an unpopulated stretch of road, and eventually they passed a small cinderblock motel. "Stop here," Stone Jay said. The boy pulled over some distance up the road, and he trudged back and went into the office. Scribbled in blue pen on the plexiglass window: *the water tastes bad*. A reply in black: *maybe its your mouth*.

The window slid open, and a stone-faced man regarded him. "We're chock-full," he said.

They drove. Clouds like smoke on a blue river. Wig store, gun store, health food store with a special on dried figs soaped to its window. A billboard advertised a motel with a hot springs on its property. *Wellspring Motel*, it read. *Be Very Well.* The boy followed the directions to it, turning several times after exiting the highway and arriving at a building with a pitched roof and a long breezeway of rooms extending from one side like a train station and a track.

"You're my nephew," Stone Jay said. "Our car got broken into."

"We were mugged," the boy said.

"No, we weren't there."

"Where were we?"

"We don't need to know that."

Inside, a woman with a puff of dyed-pink hair sat behind a desk, swiping with a cloth napkin at her small red nose. She sniffed and looked up at them, startled and pleased. Stone Jay told her their story, and she asked where they were and he said a rest stop.

"At your most vulnerable," she said. "Well, you've come to the right place. It's not like I don't have the room."

He said if he could use her address, his bank would mail him a new ATM card, stumbling a little over the phrase. He didn't have an ATM card. He didn't have a bank account. He lived beneath the surface of respectability. He could see it above him sometimes, as if in a nightmare where a glass pane was lowered over a pool he swam in, trapping him underwater.

He entered a small bathroom off the lobby. In the mirror, his eyes were a needy blue, porous, floating.

Back in the lobby, he stood looking out a sliding glass door at the springs, which were a trio of round concrete pools of ascending size fed by an exposed pipe. A beer bottle stood by the smallest, its label flaked around its base. He thought then to check under his fingernails for blood. It was there, tar-dark, and he stood with his hands splayed in front of him incredulously, drawing them into fists only after the woman returned with keys.

THE BOY

There was a razor in the medicine cabinet of the room he was given. He used the hard little bar of soap to lather his face, then drew the razor across his chin. Powdery stubble stuck to bubbles and fell into the sink. When he was done he splashed water at the soap scum and checked in the mirror to see if he was bleeding. You could feel sorry for a boy but not for a man, and since he looked like a boy, they might as well feel sorry for him. He looked like poverty, a point of inconsequence pinned to the earth. He looked like crooked teeth. He looked like skinny limbs. He looked like an aluminum scrap of wind. At eighteen he looked twelve. Did he mean to do it? Day after day of boredom. Day after day of ugliness. Bulk bags of rubber bands, his grandmother rolling her mailers in front of the TV. Big deal pre-sale freshwater strands of forever memories lunchtime special statement earrings. The saleswomen rotated their wrists slowly and tilted their heads almost indiscernibly sideways so their chattering jewelry caught the light. They looked as if they were listening for instructions from a distant source, poised on the brink of an engulfing subservience, and his grandmother must've objected to them even as she let them in. Daytime shine nighttime spark. Celebrate your tomorrows today. He was tired of being himself. Did his grandmother feel the same way? Gape-jawed in front of the screen, watching one woman on tiptoe model a pair of boots, another caress a tennis bracelet.

ELENA

Yes and no, departing guests used to say when she asked them if they'd enjoyed their stay. Yes and no. If she urged them to explain, they demurred or seemed offended, so she started leaving index cards in the rooms that read, Help Us Do Better.

The springs were not natural seeming. They were hottubesque.

The hostess was forward in a way I found uncomfortable to ascertain.

No bacon, good coffee.

I didn't expect luxury but I expected a clean healing kind of crystals place or something.

If you agree with Kant's assertion that morality is not the doctrine of how we make ourselves happy, but how we make ourselves worthy of happiness, then what are you doing here?

At this point in time I would not return.

She assumed those who left no comment had been pleased with their experience, for it was human nature to be wordy in complaint and silent in contentment. Still, she would've liked a little pat on the back every now and then, and took the blank cards as such. She was losing business to resorts whose glossy advertisements featured dangling strands of succulents like fat jeweled necklaces, aloe in clay pots. People loved clay pots. The human appreciation for clay pots seemed nearly unquenchable, but she could not coax anything to grow in a pot or even keep what was already alive alive. It turned out you *could* kill cacti, or at least they could go brown and split-tipped and list to the side in that remote, remonstrative way plants had.

Once, she'd heard a little girl say to her father as they lolled before the jets, "When I get older I'm going to have a bodyguard and I'm going to tell my bodyguard to kill me."

The girl seemed perfectly cheery, leapfrogging over lounge chairs. There hadn't been any guests for some time now, some weeks.

Both of her exes had had children before she met them. Todd, Gavin, Tanner, Neil, Hunter. Todd and Gavin belonged to her first husband, Tanner, Neil, and Hunter to the second. Neil cowed a little before Tanner and Hunter, she remembered. She used to buy them Nerf guns and squishy orange ammo for their birthdays, but now she couldn't even say how old they were. You could vanish that way from the world, bit by bit from the minds of those who let you go. It was gentle, the motion, like a hand opening to release a bit of sand.

Boys to whom she'd once given gifts now ageless, fading.

She wondered if she'd recognize them in a grocery store. Surely they'd recognize her as the woman with whom their fathers had had brief, confusing marriages. Their fathers and the woman had seemed so happy some days and so downtrodden others. It had been like watching an uneven game of Ping-Pong. The ball was hollow, light as a feather. It rolled under things and got stuck.

Her second ex owned the motel, and after they'd divorced it was decided she'd stay on. She paid him rent on it. Having been freed from responsibility for the place, he charged her only half of what he could.

What her first husband said when she suggested they get married: That would make sense. What her second husband said: Why not? There was an undeniable element of casualness to the exchanges. She had hoped that quality would keep them fresh, unspoiled by the architecture of courtship. That she had been the one to suggest it both times bothered her only slightly. She had seen it suddenly—they could be married, could entertain each other with stories of their little trials and tribulations at the end of the day—and her future husbands had been flattered, she thought, when really she was just saying some words, testing out a possible arrangement. People made too big a deal of these things. Was it lightness she was after? Or a certain detachment that would make the parting easier? Her husbands had not wanted to hear about her trials and tribulations even when relayed entertainingly. Her first husband liked to listen to Paul Simon and eat salt-and-vinegar chips. Her second husband liked to listen to Pavement and drink mescal cocktails. She knew them, and they knew her, and that they'd decided to go their separate ways was an indictment of that knowing and an odd sort of affirmation of it, a strangely honest regard. It said, *I know what you're going to be like for the next thirty years. I've seen your present and you've told me at length about your past and based on that, I can predict*—and the thought would sit in her head that way, whirring like a dying instrument, because the future was unknowable. To become was a process of unbecoming by which each abandoned thing gave shape to the original. She had married once and then again, and, after the second marriage ended, acknowledged to herself that it would probably be her last. Subtle, solid knowledge, but if you were your only confidant, did it matter? Did it even count?

WILSON

He went to his desk. The view out the window was of the long breathing mountains. All his pretty days of striving were behind him. His first semester at Monroe, in an act of misguided egalitarianism, he'd distributed one of his own poems to be workshopped by his class, and a student had returned it scrawled with *You kind of sound like a teenage boy with a hardon. I have never used the word hardon before so forgive me if it is misspelled.* Felicity Pike. She sat with arms and legs crossed, her tidy body a reproof to men like him, who failed to see the dark line that ran through them like a mud vein in a shrimp. Her face seethed with intelligence one moment and hostility the next, daring him to bother her for her opinion. He dared not, then worried he wasn't pushing her enough.

Felicity, he said anxiously as she packed up after class.

She gazed at him, bangs twitching as she blinked.

Did you have a question?

Not at all, she said.

If being in proximity to others brought you into proximity to yourself, did it follow that *you* were the source of every scattered woe, every slight or snub or awkwardness? The campus had a computer center filled with big new Macs, and once, after meeting a student there, he'd jostled a chair that jostled a mouse that caused a screen to blink on to CAN THONGS GIVE YOU CANCER in a search bar. Poor humans. Poor him, who knew they could not, though of course there was so much else that could. The danger was being afraid of the wrong thing. The danger was having your eye on the wrong thing while the right thing had its eye on you. He had never gotten hit by a car. He had had no melanomas. His heart ticked along. But he knew there was a place where cars and cells and hearts lost control, and it was very nearby. It was in the mirror, his own life's double image. Waiting, waiting for him to see it.

How far he'd come. He used to see a man in the mirror. He used to be easily tricked.

He got up and turned off the light and locked the door. The danger was here.

Audrey had a tendency to lie perfectly still during sex, so once the thought that he was fucking a cold wedge of Swiss cheese popped into his head, he couldn't purge that image. She was not a post-sex crier, contemplator, or analyzer. She went into the bathroom and peed with great velocity and came back to bed and fell asleep. It was he who lay awake and regretted that she'd been with only one other person (and even then he suspected she might have invented him, Lars Someone from Denmark). He wanted her to have experienced more, to have had a more varied past, and while he told himself this thought was born of love and generosity, really it was to take some of the pressure off of him. He wished she'd had a prospect in the class of his she'd taken, someone who'd pursued her, made her feel good. He wasn't sure if he ever made her feel good.

He found mention of their sex life in her calendar once. She treated the calendar like a journal, writing a short entry in each day's square, and occasionally, when he was bored, he'd take a look. *Inhaled a chunk of 100 Grand bar* one would say, or, *I think babies think I'm ugly.* The doozy, the entry about their conjugal relations, read, *I'm tempted to say W hates having sex with me. Does it out of guilt, obligation. It's just orifice hunting to him. Where's the passion?*

This was terrible for two reasons. First, orifice hunting: it implied being lost, a state of fumbling ineptitude, or, worse, the act of tracking and killing, neither of which he thought accurately described him in bed. He was if anything rather careful and sedate, solicitous, distantly curious, as if examining pieces in a museum case. And second: now his hands were tied—he couldn't start being more affectionate without Audrey suspecting he'd snooped. Maybe it was a test. Maybe neither of them worshipped each other's bodies like they should. She wasn't comfy, didn't nestle softly against him, a series of dips and swells. She was all angle and bone—hips, ribs, spine.

He was the opposite, with a pudgy stomach and a hairy chest, and hair on his back in the shape of a bell.

Maybe it was all a sham. Maybe Audrey hadn't expected him to accept her advances. Shortly after she asked him out for coffee, a book buyer named Khondamir had walked in on them making out in his office, Khondamir who trawled the halls of Monroe knocking discreetly on professors' doors and buying textbooks for cash, a hurried transaction whose pleasure was simple—free anthologies arrived in the mail, enticements for your syllabi, but if you decided against using them, they were yours for the selling, and everyone turned a profit but Norton, poor thing. The knock had been followed not by a pause but by Khondamir pushing open his cracked door, which told him that based on the many sample anthologies he'd sold, Khondamir considered him a friend, someone whose mostly closed door could be breached. Excuse! Khondamir exclaimed, and Wilson jumped to his feet, sending Audrey tumbling to the floor. He imagined the atrocities Khondamir might've witnessed in his native country, and how laughable this transgression must seem, how it might be something he'd reenact later for other book buyers, only exaggeratedly, pitying the lust involved, the need. Khondamir had a hard, lithe shell that prevented anything as squishy as need from showing, anything as simple. It was Khondamir who'd extended a hand to Audrey to help her up, and she thanked him extravagantly, as if she knew she had to be gracious for them both. Ten months later, she and Wilson were married at City Hall. Afterward, in the warm spring air, he plucked from her hand the plastic bag the clerk had given her that contained sample-sized detergents and a ball of steel wool, and stood on tiptoe to throw it in a high, freewheeling arc into a trash can. She cried out in surprise and delight, as euphoric as he'd ever seen her—middle of the afternoon in her white flapper's dress with silk fringe—because, he realized later, she thought he'd miss. She was sure of it!

She got her realtor's license, and he continued teaching students who were just a few years younger than she, and then more than a few years. They fought about insubstantial things, and he came away with insubstantial victories, but on the more serious subject of whether or not to have children, she triumphed completely. They drove a small red car with a racing stripe; the phrase *maternity clothes* made her shudder; she was precise, obsessive, hard on herself, and wouldn't take to the inevitable chaos and mess children would bring—but still he wondered, every now and then, what a child of theirs would've looked like, who he or she would've been. There were a million options, he figured, but he couldn't imagine even one.

ELENA

He was like a puppet you operated with sticks. His limbs seemed to dangle too far apart and his shoulders were high and unnaturally stiff. She asked the boy if he was hungry, and he shrugged, twitch of a string. She led him to the kitchen and made a peanut butter and honey sandwich and watched him chew, watched his thin throat twist down wads of food. "Have another, have another," she urged, feeling there was no better encouragement. She remembered traveling to Greece as a teenager, ten or so years after she'd first visited, and her aunt making a gesture about her that Elena wasn't meant to see, billowing out her cheeks like a tuba player—she's gotten fat, eh? She logged every bite of fish Elena took, every fried potato. Elena snuck down to the square at night and bought apple pastries. The air was warm, and people stayed up late laughing and talking. She carried her Susan Sontag with her and read as she ate, an uptight American. The only interesting answers are the ones that destroy the question, Sontag wrote, and Elena wished her aunt would discover her coming back up in the grated elevator and ask her what she was doing. She wanted to destroy her aunt's disapproval, how she thought that because Elena was a girl she shouldn't want, shouldn't need, shouldn't conduct herself according to her own wishes, shouldn't satisfy herself but always wait and wonder and deny, doubt, go without, stand by the stove as the men ate and smoked, remain silent and hungry. She wanted to say *I was stuffing my face*. Chocolates and loukoumi—

sticky-sweet squares of fruit-flavored gelatin dusted with powdered sugar—and Orangina on the ferry.

On Cephalonia, the island where her father was born, a bee stung her above her right eye as she stood looking over her father's cousin's hives. Her parents and brother had been given veils, but since Elena was allergic she had stayed back. The cousin, not understanding, drew forth the honeycomb and brought it to her, golden city furred with bees, the betrayed swarm following.

WILSON

In his email inbox, Monroe College welcomed rapper Frohawk Two Feathers to campus, and Monroe's Department of English invited students, faculty, and staff to a reading by Summer Truttmann, newly appointed Assistant Professor of Creative Writing. Wilson was the one who'd first brought her to Monroe. She was an ecopoet known for her interviews with trees. On the page, these interviews took the shape of a series of questions such as *Your leaves drop to the earth and blow away. New leaves grow. Is there a difference between renewal and replication?* or *Is wildfire a beginning or an end?* interspersed with the tree's answers, long lines of SSSSSSs and TTTTTTs and HOOOOs and barbed-wire clusters of hyphens and colons and pound signs that seemed to indicate that the interviewee was a hissing and profane being, or rendered wordless by the inanity of the questions. She called her poems arboreal hieroglyphics.

They didn't sleep together during that visit, though they engaged in a kind of verbal foreplay and arranged to meet again at a writers' conference, where among the small but ardent crowds her readings drew she was treated like royalty. The audience leaned forward in their seats as she read, as if they'd all come down with stomach cramps. She performed her poems with such a straight face that he began to take them seriously too. *You've been touched by the violence of chainsaws. How do you forgive?* the ecopoet asked, and he strained to hear the poor old oak's answer.

Afterward, he sat next to her as she signed books. She signed the same thing every time. *For P.—I don't know you, but I'm sure you're very brave. For C.—I don't know you, but I'm sure you're very brave. For T.—I don't know you, but I'm sure you're very brave. For S.—I don't know you, but I'm sure you're very*—and here she stayed her hand, letting ink pool on the creamy paper from the tip of her pen. What would she write instead? Smart? Confident? Witty? Generous? She wrote *sane,* slammed the book shut, and stood up. She wore a knee-baring midnight-blue dress and high-heeled boots that were not, she had gone to some pains to explain, real leather. They went to the hotel bar and ordered a drink.

And after all the readings and panels and assorted bullshit events are over, you know what I like to do? Eat a Twix in bed, someone sitting near them said, to which her companion made a prolonged sound of orgasmic agreement. The ecopoet rolled her eyes and said she was craving a cigarette, so they drank their gin and tonics very quickly and went out the hotel's revolving door into the hideous cold. It was Chicago (these conferences always seemed to be in Chicago), and the wind threw the smoke from her American Spirit straight into his face. People came up to congratulate her on her reading, and he noted how she accepted praise without deflecting or dodging or demurring, how artful she was in basking. You have to believe in yourself, he thought, before anyone else will. Yeah, yeah, something like that, though so far his belief in himself took the form of a tiny room he defiled with his uncertainty. His feet felt like blocks of ice. Finally they went back inside, and the avidity with which they embraced the warmth turned into the avidity with which they embraced each other. The ecopoet revealed a predilection for being on top, and a long scar across her abdomen from a fall from a eucalyptus tree. She revealed a predilection for room-service hamburgers that ran contrary to her public persona. Living was cheating on the life you were supposed to have, she pronounced casually. She pushed her empty plate away and sprang on him again, but he couldn't enjoy himself, distracted by the thought that she might spew that chewed-up flesh out of her mouth to splatter against the padded white headboard and drip down onto the long white pillows, distracted by her chortles of pleasure and the sound their bodies made slapping together, a draining-bathtub sound, and when he finally felt himself quake and shudder, a strange melancholy went through him, as if he'd lost something he didn't want to give.

Now she'd gotten the job that should've been his, but he would not let her know it.

The little incidents. The creeping indignities. A business card tucked next to his bill at a pierogi restaurant. *Lucky Good Hands. Swedish hot stone deep tissue sensual massage.* On the back of the card, written in purple ink, the name Ruth. Driving home, tires moaning. Coming in the door to an empty house, dialing the number.

"Lucky good hands," a woman answered.

"What makes you lucky?"

"Total knowledge and service. You wanna book?"

"Is this Ruth?"

"Sure it's Ruth."

He laughed weakly. "Well, Ruth, what are you wearing?"

"Lab coat and heels."

He went into the bedroom. "And underneath?"

"Just skin, sweetheart. You wanna book or not?"

He made an appointment under the name Steve Ladder.

"I'll climb your ladder," the woman said.

For the first time in the exchange he felt a stirring of arousal. "Okay," he said shyly, wondering how it was people did this.

"You wanna pay for phone sex now?"

"Oh, no, I can't. Sorry."

The woman ignored him, lowering her voice to a hoarse whisper and speaking rapidly. "Putyercockinoutinoutinoutrealfast."

He sat on the edge of the bed.

"Like it?"

He shrugged, then realized she couldn't see him. *He* could see him; that was the problem. He was somehow both insignificant and obscenely large, like a fleshy Galápagos tortoise. "I can't pretend. I'm sorry."

"Don't pretend!"

He blushed, but his interest was piqued, he couldn't deny it. "Just a second." His gaze landed on a tank top of Audrey's, a limp black thing tangled in the bedding. He locked the door, unzipped his zipper, and took himself in his hand. His penis was like the thumb of a leather glove. He put the phone on speaker. "Okay," he said. "What now?"

"You a virgin?"

"Yeah." It was true, in a way.

She proceeded to describe exactly what he should do to her as if she were reciting a recipe for something that involved a lot of stirring, like risotto. As he listened he mashed the tank top to his face, breathing in its sweaty, skin-of-scrambled-eggs smell, and then held it to his crotch and moved it around a little. He felt flimsy, unacted upon, caught at a dulling distance from the event that was unfolding. The phone sex. The way she said inoutinoutinout so quickly, it came out sounding like now, now, now, now.

"I've got to go," he said suddenly.

"What? You owe me fifty-two fifty, asshole."

He hung up. He was embarrassed for himself, for the walls that had witnessed him. He was embarrassed for the woman who was or was not Ruth. The mechanical weight she lifted just by being. And scared of her, too, of her disdain. To find himself wanting disdain, anything. To find himself at the command of a voice that didn't know him, nor he it. Where did it come from? Where did it sleep at night? Strangers had always had this power over him, the power of how little he knew about them, of how obedient he could be to the unknown.

He folded the tank top and then remembered how he'd found it, unfolded it, and flung it back onto the bed.

ELENA

A tweet by a woman whose fingerprints had been stolen led her to a tweet by a woman who listed all the animals men had compared her to (buffalo, hippo, panda, goat) led her to a tweet by a woman who quoted Kate Millett on Norman Mailer's masculinity ("precarious spiritual capital in endless need of replenishment and threatened on every side") led her to a tweet by a woman who thought white women should not wear hoop earrings led her to a tweet by a woman who made her own soap led her to a tweet by a woman who'd forgotten a tampon inside her for three-and-a-half years and when it emerged looked like a burnt finger led her to a tweet by a woman whose plumber had stood in her kitchen and ripped up the card of another plumber he'd found there led her to a tweet by a woman who collected beer bottle tops for mixed-media art projects led her to a tweet by a woman who'd worked with soft serve and thereafter could never eat soft serve again led her to a tweet by a woman who'd gone to a lot of punk shows in L.A. in the '80s and had noticed, in a book later published about the scene, a photograph of her hands with a caption that read *Man's Hands*.

She ran into her second ex coming around the side of the motel, drying his hands on his jeans. He was a broad-shouldered man with ruddy sideburns and an expression of remorseful intent. "I reset the sprinklers," he said. "Shaved off a minute."

"Great," she said. "Want some coffee?"

He followed her into the kitchen. "Listen, I need to talk a time table with you. How long you can go on like this."

She started to speak, and he raised his voice over hers. "Yes, I see there's someone here now—"

"Two someones, actually."

"But we both know it's been slim pickings."

"The way you put things," she said. "It's indiscriminate."

"Elena," he said. "I'm just stating a fact."

She had gone into this marriage assuming she'd worked out the kinks the first time around, only to find her second experience as baffling and muddled, possibly more so. Her husbands—both of them—had erected walls in front of her intentions, in front of her deepest desires, ideas she hoped to nurture and make flesh: to have lively dinner table conversation, to tell stories with her possessions (Remember how I haggled, in my high school Spanish, for these earrings at that market in Mérida?), to create the atmosphere for intimacy, for an unburdening of minds. The décor was rattan furniture and batik spreads and nature's detritus—scattered acorns and pinecones and pebbles that had shone so beguilingly in their riverbeds but were chalky on the shelves, dulled. A tumbleweed hung over the reception desk. You appreciated how huge they were when rescued from the road and brought inside.

The most intimate thing her second ex had ever told her was that his barber had said he had cat hair.

Now he got up from the table and came toward her. Was he going to touch her?

He reached past her to empty his mug into the sink. "What it is, is time's ticking," he said.

She had thought he contained a hidden complexity that just had to be coaxed out. For many years, she had thought of herself as the coaxer-outer of the hidden complexities of men. First they would kiss her breasts, and then they would be moved to confession, self-reflection. . . .

"That's a terrible way to think about it," she said. "About time. I like that it passes. I wouldn't mind if it passed more quickly. What's there to be afraid of?"

His expression became practiced. She supposed he'd heard this before.

Still, she pressed on. "I'm not afraid of getting old, or ugly, for that matter. Beauty's boring."

She was forty-four and certain of it, as certain as she could be. There was a postcard magneted to the refrigerator that showed a bridge strung with lights, the silky Danube. *Dear Elena*, it read, *Here in Budapest I think I might explode into a shrapnel of happiness. It is too much for one man to bear. I will try to bear it.* She had thought for a time that its author might be husband number three, but he had the travel bug, and she couldn't easily leave, and in any case he had not invited her. It had shaken her, not being invited. They had pawed at each other brusquely, but she had hoped there was something else there, the kind of pleasure that would demand continuation. He had fastened her wrists to her headboard with her orange-sherbet-colored scarf.

"I'm not talking about beauty," her second ex said. "I'm not really even talking about you."

But the motel was her, and she it, and she opened her mouth to say so and then thought better of it. He would remind her that he was the owner, and in regard to her being, she didn't want to consider ownership.

THE BOY

He was sitting in the motel's small kitchen with Stone Jay and the proprietor, the parts of a meal she'd invited them to share spread out on the table before them, black beans and rice and peppers and grated cheese to be tucked into tortillas kept warm in a tortilla-shaped container. She said before they dug in they should go around and say one good thing that'd happened to them that day. For example, she'd thought the garbage disposal was broken but it turned out not to be.

Dying succulent on the windowsill. Stick of smoking incense that smelled like the air freshener (Garlands of Lilacs) his grandmother had used. He could picture the aerosol can sitting on the toilet tank, economy-sized, as if in endless demand. They were forever running out of things (bread, milk, margarine, macaroni), but they always had a mist to spray in the bathroom, one odor to cover up another, more truculent odor. His grandmother was oddly fastidious about things like that. She kept herself clean even as his hair went unwashed, his teeth unbrushed. Her braid braided so tightly it shone, the bottom-most button of a camel-colored cardigan she wore over a black POW MIA t-shirt always buttoned.

His good thing, Stone Jay said, was meeting someone as generous as she'd been to them, even though, he added, he hadn't met her specifically that day. "It reverberates," he said.

"That's sweet," she said as Stone Jay busied himself loading up a tortilla.

She turned to the boy. "What about you?"

"Can it be last night?'

"Alright."

"I dreamed my grandmother was well again."

"Was she sick?"

"She is sick," he said.

"Was it a very vivid dream?"

"Vivid in the sense of dreams, like dreams are. I can't describe it."

"No." She looked disappointed. "People rarely can. But your parents, where are they?"

"They're not around. They died when I was a baby. It's fine," he said quickly. "I'm used to it." He'd had teachers like her, who'd slip him school supplies on the sly, bring him blueberry muffins and banana bread, try to get him to confide in them. Their eyes crinkly, empathetic, a little sad, like balled-up wrapping paper. But his grandmother had coached him well, and he had confided nothing. She had cultivated in him a disdain for other people that he knew served her purposes—if he was close to no one, he'd have no one to go to, no one to turn to in need. He'd had some friendships growing up, but they didn't run very deep.

She was asking Stone Jay a question. ". . . ever since?"

"After his grandmother stopped being able to. Isn't that right?" Stone Jay took a big bite, and beans dribbled out of his tortilla. "Ask him."

"Yeah, after that," the boy said.

"I didn't have much to do with her. She didn't like me very much," Stone Jay said.

He was trying to draw the boy into elaborating. He still felt guilty for leaving her and was being stupid, sloppy.

"Why didn't she like you, if you don't mind me asking?"

"She didn't really like men," the boy said.

"Oh?"

"I think she wanted to start over. Start again where there wouldn't be this order to things."

"Order."

"This system in place. My grandmother saw it more clearly than most people."

"What does it look like? No, don't tell me. I'll see it everywhere if you do." The proprietor reared up from the table and began to clear dishes, even though Stone Jay was the only one who'd eaten anything. "Can I tempt either of you with some nondairy mint chocolate chip?"

It was white instead of green, and it tasted of chalk. The boy ate a bowl while she ran the water and rattled at the sink, a faraway sound, comforting.

WILSON

His leg was asleep. He shifted in the chair but did not get up, for he was afraid if he did some tentacle of the logical world would wrap around him and drag him above. Syllabi for the class he was no longer teaching sat stacked in the upper right corner of his desk. Under FURTHER MATTERS he'd written, *Converse with the text. What do I mean by that? Question its parts, question its decisions, question its relevance. Who is the speaker of the poem? Probably your classmate. What do they want? Probably a job with a dot com. Probably an app to think for them, to read for them, to accumulate the knowledge you should get by living. Are you people even having sex anymore? Put another way: can you make poetry out of passivity, spectatorship, "liking" things on Instagram? Or, the flipside, shallow showmanship, posting things on your "story"? (That's OUR language, by the way, the language of writers.) What enables these behaviors is screens, which is why I'm banning phones and computers in and around this class. Everything you write, you'll write longhand.*

He dropped the stack into the recycling container and looked around his office—bookshelves, French press and bag of ground coffee, coat rack and straw fedora, vintage advertisement for Sunkist with a round-faced woman smiling under a branch of bulbous oranges—and then into his desk drawers, where the instruments of salvation grew smaller but more necessary: breath mints, bottles of airplane gin, Xanax, note. Handwritten, so there was that.

He could hear Midge telling a student that no, she would not be available to edit his personal statement for his application to a top entertainment PR firm.

Gone the reticence. Gone the reverence and awe, the small gestures of genuflection—gone the way of CD players and flannel shirts. Even seeking advice was dated. Seeking advice was such an innocent thing, implying that one's future may be an open field, undecided, sloping and uneven. What students wanted now were connections, favors. A path forward as smooth as a putting green.

There was a knock on his door. It must be Midge, wanting to commiserate, but he couldn't, he wouldn't. His outrage was thin and watery; it was pooling at his feet.

Leaving him empty. And so porous that for a moment he seriously reconsidered. He held still as she leaned against the door. He could hear her necklace scraping the wood, the puffing of her breath, the crinkly butting of her hair. He had sisters like her, unabashed arrangements of parts that operated under the edicts of knowledgeable, judgmental brains. Midge was in her sixties, and he wanted to be younger than someone for a change. To be positioned in a place of greater possibility. So why not open up, if only for a minute? His hand reached for the knob just as a foghorn voice in the hallway asked if he could run something by her (Greg Fogarty, Twentieth Century American Lit), and she said of course and gave one last rap and it would be mistake for him to read anything into the rap other than a bland request for his presence, but it sounded a little more prescient than that, it had an undertone of inquiry to it, like it knew—or suspected!—what he was up to, and the fact that even so (possibly so, maybe so) she turned away hurt him more than, much more than, was rational.

His office was among the smallest in Hancock Hall. Perhaps *the* smallest. Life was a numbers game. Square feet, how many students lined up outside his door during office hours, how many books he'd published, how many children he had, how many miles his car got to the gallon, how long it took for people to email him back, how often he had sex with his wife, what the scale said, how long he'd been on Earth, who would miss him when he was gone. For years he had waited to be made faculty editor of *Comeuppance: A Literary Journal*, patiently at first, then with a bone-jabbering impatience that became anger that became paranoia that became dread that became, finally, defeat that told him he didn't deserve to be made faculty editor of *Comeuppance: A Literary Journal*, anyway. The parts of his work that should've been true were false and the parts that should've been false were true. Correctable, if you had the will. The problem with will was it required itself to sustain itself, like a fire that needed fire to burn. He took off his shoes and socks and sat breathing deeply. His note read *This was not the way, not the vehicle by which nor the venue in which to convey anything with any accuracy.* Words were cheap. Words were holy. Well, which was it? After his mother died, her lawyer had convened a meeting of him and his three sisters to inform them that her estate had been split evenly four ways. There had been no getting into who needed what or who had expressed a fondness for this or that marble-topped curio table. Paper-clipped to her will, on her monogrammed stationery: *You were a jolly gang.* His sisters were miffed not to be recognized individually, but he knew at the end it was better for her to think of them this way, just as it was better for him to let the specifics go. He had lived in a place with palm trees. He had lived where the sun was a blade whining down through a piece of wood, and he had showered in its dust.

He was not a showman, the type to jump from a roof. He took a handful of Xanax with the airplane gin, pushed his chair back from his desk and crawled beneath it. The pills were pale peach, a child's color. His head was a glass orb, a glass eye. If EMTs surged in and hauled him away to the music of sirens ringing *sick man sick man*, if one pounded on his body while the other drove, if they took him to the place that ran on machinery and pumped his stomach (aquarium of ill-intentioned fish), if they could not see what he wanted or thought better of it, Stone Jay would visit, and Audrey too, and maybe they'd reconcile and maybe they wouldn't. They were like children of his, the children he'd never had. He could hope for the best for them and he could hope they got along and he could hope they were good to each other and he could hope they found peace and he could hope and hope until there was no hope left but he couldn't be responsible for the children he'd never had.

A knock again, more insistent. Cora—maybe it had been Cora all along—called, "Wilson, I'm coming in."

He tried to move, to open his eyes. Keys scrabbled in the lock, one after another until there was a neat click like a shot glass brought down onto a glass tabletop, and the door sighed open. Flick of a switch.

"Oh, god," she said and sank beside him and rested her head on his chest and farted quickly. "Can you hear me? Blink if you can hear me."

Again he tried, like thumbing a lighter and getting no flame.

Two fingers pressed his wrist, and she counted the beats then stood, hands fumbling the phone receiver—all nerves, he could tell, he could sense her vibrating—and punching in numbers and hanging up. "Wilson, what is this?" she said. "I don't understand. I wanted you to get your due. I really did. I'm not shallow, I'm not terribly egotistical, but I too feel as if I'm owed more than could ever be repaid me, and that imbalance, that tilted landscape—my landscape, your landscape, the landscape we all inhabit—that's it, don't you know? We live to redeem ourselves."

It was true there was nothing but the music of humiliation, though it had been his great act of ego to think he heard it more keenly than anyone else. La la la, it sang, dear Wilson Westing, thank you for the out of many we suggest you revisit the limit your no more than didn't believe couldn't see the forest for the—

As he was lifted onto the gurney he heard a voice say, "Watch his head." The reading had ended, and the theater was emptying. People shuffled up aisles threaded with little lights, their heads bowed, circumspect. There would be laughter and judgment later, but for now the closing words hung heavily in the air. Slowly, slowly, deciding what to say. Some knew. Others would go against the consensus, no matter what. Still others had responded with an old leaping of feeling they were ashamed of, that reminded them of their younger years, when words thrilled with their unexplored geneses, their mysterious arrangements. When they were easily impressed. But they were shrewd now, and revered nothing for fear of revering the wrong thing. Out with them, out into the night, to a noisy bar where they ordered beers and—yes, it was safest—commenced condemning, bending this way and that to avoid the pool cues of players at a nearby table, their voices raised over the music, the paternalistic disciplining structure he applied to the narrative was so obvious, like just when it might've, I don't know, taken *flight*, there was this bullying kind of finger-waggle and the old gears of plot grinding up again. . . . It began to rain. The neon sign slurred and ran. In the theater, the sound of rain on the roof perfected his aloneness. He leaned back in his seat and breathed in the mildewed smell of old velvet, then got up and mounted the steps—careful, he was groggy—and made his way across the stage to the podium, where he tapped the microphone. Bumft-bumft—the rain kept falling and now the footsteps came down.

ELENA

She was conducting an early-morning internet search of old flames. She told herself that nothing she unearthed would hurt her, not the toned wives and dazzling little children who crowded the photos of the old flames, not the wildflowers in jam jars or herb-encrusted pork roasts or the luxury of pretty bare feet. How thoroughly the wives had turned the old flames' lives picturesque, when the men themselves had been unshaven and wrinkle-shirted, pockets crinkly with receipts, toenails thick and yellowing. They'd seemed impervious to how nicely she arrayed fruit and rolls on the buffet table, liable to scrape their eyes over what she most wanted to be seen and focus on some flaw of hers, though when she asked them about her stomach or feet or calves or cheeks they claimed not to notice anything amiss. You're fine, they said, patting her offending part. You're great.

A handful of old flames remained unmarried. They were the adventurers, black-hearted and ambitious, not about to let themselves be tied down. They took photos of landscapes, not people. They belonged to groups that had the word *Action* in their titles.

She sipped her acai smoothie and typed in Stone Jay's name on a whim. The search turned up a mug shot of him as a younger man, one eye smudged a deep, bruised blue. An item in the *Fairmont Courier* police blotter, dated almost ten years ago, said he'd been booked for public intoxication and disorderliness after throwing a Kryptonite bike lock through the window of a ramen shop and urinating on West 8th Street. There was one other match, from the *Courier* again, published three days earlier. The body of Wilson Westing, longtime lecturer at Monroe College, had been found in his office on campus and transported to Pomona Valley Hospital, where he died shortly thereafter. Survived by his wife, Audrey Billingsley, and brother-in-law, Jay Billingsley, both Fairmont residents, it read, and went on to list the names of siblings who lived out of state.

This was no good. This was very bad. Nervously, she clicked to another page where rain barrels were for sale and the copy center was hiring if you knew how to troubleshoot copy machinery, and then returned to the notice after willing it to have disappeared. It was still there. She shut her laptop. She had been to Fairmont once with her first husband. They'd had lunch at an overpriced Italian restaurant and wandered the college campus, passing under bowers of blooming vines and through courtyards with hushed, trembling fountains. Signs implored students to avail themselves of complimentary tea and scones from the tea carts, and stress-relieving puppy-petting sessions in the student center.

She and her husband had met at community college, in a classroom in which thirty-eight students sat crammed behind blue plastic desks, a tide of Ding Dong wrappers at their ankles.

She thought she understood Stone Jay a little. His pissing down that prosperous street.

Should she not give him the news? Should she let him steep in ignorance a while longer? She had been nosy and bored, snooping around online (though in regard to Stone Jay you could say she was doing due diligence), and now the news was hers to tell.

STONE JAY

Yards of trucks. Yards of sand. A yard of geodesic domes. Sidewalk-less streets, streets where the asphalt broke down to black crumbs. Dead agave pulled onto its side by the weight of its stalk, small new green agave sprouting beneath it. Blossoms on cacti like crepe-paper thumbprints. Dreamcatcher rearview-mirror ornaments and 4x4 trucks, tire treads reptilian in the dust. Trash in scrub and weeds and cholla, paper coffee cups and crushed beer cans, latex glove like a crumpled starfish. In the distance, turbines turning, turbines standing still. Pink smoke of sunrise that spread and softened on the shoulders of the unbeautiful, the abandoned and forlorn, chest of drawers facedown in the dirt, claps of barking dogs. The desert everywhere around him, inside him. When he returned to the motel Elena was waiting for him.

He sat in the backseat of the Lyft she'd called for him, staring out the window. The future was here, broken-glass dazzle of sky, slick machinery for hire pulsing forward over a black snake of road. The transaction conducted on screen, wordlessly, and now he rode with a stranger, silent and at his mercy. And wasn't one of the things about the future how little mercy there would be? The driver slowed and edged into a chaotic intersection of roundabouts. "You okay with me stopping for a date shake?" he asked.

"I guess so," Stone Jay said. He stayed in the car, hand on door handle to make sure it would open. Fiddling it up and down. You couldn't get outside yourself very often, you couldn't escape yourself, and maybe that's what Wilson had been trying to do. It had to have been a mistake. The world was made of mistakes. . . .

The driver returned with a large shake for himself and a small one for Stone Jay. He had no appetite, but he appreciated the gesture. "Thanks," he said, and took a sip, and began talking about Wilson. He said Wilson had been like a father figure to him, even though Wilson was married to Stone Jay's sister, and that he'd only ever wanted to be part of their family. He'd wanted the freedom to belong more than the belonging. There was freedom from and freedom to, and they weren't the same thing at all, they were very, very different.

"Word," the driver said, steering them around big-rig tire shreds. They passed a gym called Crunches. They passed mountains like heaps of ashes. The driver's phone told him to take the next exit, and they looped down and around, and everything was familiar yet he could tell his estrangement had changed. There was melancholy in it, not anger. Flowers blared from yards and overwatered grass lay thick as green velvet and tree branches knit together over the streets to create blinking tunnels of shade, house and car, house and two cars, it was all very handsome and boring—he had never fit in here, never belonged, though of course he'd never wanted to belong, he'd wanted the rejection to be complete because anything else left him sour with longing. A tawny dog raised its leg against a jacaranda tree. In the park across from Audrey's house, a young man operated a drone, guiding the thing high into the air, his attention fixed as his body veered around beneath it. It was a miraculous bird he saw, black and seething. Its whine approximated the feeling in Stone Jay's chest, who realized that he was bound now to his sister through something more lasting than desperation. He was bound to her through grief.

Wilson's service took place at the Quaker meeting house. Next to the door was a basket of lemons, with a sign propped in front of it that read *Fruit Not Bombs*. "I admire the sentiment," a woman said from behind him, "though the two aren't exactly interchangeable."

It took him a second to realize she was speaking to him.

"We shall shower our enemies with citrus?" she continued as they moved inside and found seats on folding chairs set up in a circle. "Not likely. So how did you know Wilson? I was his boss, so to speak. In academia, we don't use words like boss, but I was the chair of the department where he taught."

"He was married to my sister," Stone Jay said.

"I can't believe he's dead. Every bone in my body rebels against the thought."

A blown-up picture of Wilson was propped on an easel in the middle of the circle. In it, he stood at the front of a classroom gesturing with his hands. On a desk in the corner of the frame was a glass bottle that Stone Jay recognized as an iced Starbucks frappuccino. It seemed a shame it had been memorialized in the photograph with him. It was a fleeting thing, probably some student's, and had been paired with Wilson forever, would accompany him always in the minds of those assembled and in the velvet reaches of the memories of the departed. Audrey stood up and thanked everyone for coming, and said Wilson had been her mentor and lover and husband, in that order. The woman next to him coughed. They had grown apart of late, Audrey said, but his death had brought them back together, and she held him in internal regard. Her face twitched. Eternal, she meant to say. She was incredibly nervous, so please excuse her. She sat down with a thump.

The woman sitting next to him stood. She said she'd known Wilson in a different capacity, that he'd been her loyal adjunct at Monroe College, and she had been very sorry to see him leave his teaching position, though she understood why he did. He was a poet of immense promise, a better poet than many people realized, and had been working on a very important book. She'd meant to bring one of his poems to read, but she had left it at the gym. She sat down.

There were a few apologetic coughs. A young man on the opposite side of the circle got to his feet. He said Wilson had been a super influential professor of his. He'd thought himself cut from John Berryman cloth, but Wilson had showed him he was more a snippet of Robert Frost. "It was stylistic whiplash, to be sure, but it was good for me," he said.

Stone Jay left the circle and went out back and sat on a bench on a small, kidney-bean-shaped patch of grass. A few minutes later, Audrey came and sat next to him.

She lit a cigarette. "Wilson would be shocked," she said. She took one drag and ground the cigarette out.

"You don't have to—"

"I know. It gives me something to do other than be sad. The proper display of sadness is exhausting, but if you stop for even a second people think you're a monster."

"Shocked at you smoking or shocked at the service?" he asked.

"Me smoking. The service would be unthinkable. Who could imagine it?"

People began filing past them to the tables of food set back in the garden, and it seemed to him that something moved them unerringly toward nourishment—if not the imagining of their own end, then the desire not to.

"He tried to get comfort wherever he could take it," one woman said to another.

"You mean *take comfort*—I know what you mean," the other woman said.

The former student of Wilson's swerved away from the group and came over. He wore a crisp white shirt and red suspenders.

"Mrs. Westing?" he said to Audrey. "I wanted you to know he talked about you. I came to his office hours pretty faithfully. We hung out together, intellectually speaking."

"Once upon a time, I was his student, too," she said.

"We were his protégés!" The young man's face grew reverent. "Did he shape your aesthetic the way he shaped mine? I desperately needed shaping. I come from a family of nonreaders. My dad used to stand out in the driveway, leaf-blowing in the rain."

"That's quite an image."

"I've tried writing about it, but I can't get it right. It wasn't a sad sight. It was his stubbornness that struck—"

In the middle of his sentence, she wandered over to the food table and plucked a spanakopita from a platter.

The young man looked crestfallen.

"It's not you," Stone Jay said to him. "She's upset."

He nodded quickly, looping his thumbs under the suspenders, obviously grateful to have them.

Audrey was no longer at the food table. She wasn't standing in any of the clusters of guests, or smoking a cigarette at the side of the yard. Finally he found her in the meeting house's kitchen, washing her hands very thoroughly, her untouched spanakopita next to the sink. She flicked her fingers at the window and spoke to her reflection.

"This is my husband we're talking about! He wanted nothing to do with you. He thought you were . . ."

"What?" Stone Jay said.

"Taking advantage again."

When they were children he used to go into her room looking to wreak havoc. Once, he found lined up on her windowsill a row of little tinfoil cups and plates and spoons and forks that she'd made for her dollhouse, delicate glinting things, imagine spending your time doing that, imagine the care, the contentment, the self-satisfaction . . . He swept them to the floor and crushed them under his feet. If he could not imagine, he could destroy. They flattened easily into something like gum wrappers.

"I'm sorry," he said now, but she was already heading out of the kitchen. "Audrey," he called. She paused at the door. She didn't turn around.

"He can't have meant it, can he?"

"I don't know," she said. "What do you think?"

AUDREY

Shortly after the service, she received a card from her mother. She went into the bathroom and sat on the side of the tub to run the water. As the tub filled, she tore open the envelope and read the message quickly—*I'm so sorry for your lost*—the words nearly illegible in her mother's arthritic hand. What else is she sorry for? she thought with sudden bitterness. She turned the faucet off and the showerhead on, stripped, and stepped into an inch of hot water. The showerhead was removable. She aimed it between her legs.

A poetry workshop at a small liberal arts college: picture a huddle of stunning creatures, young and loud in their youngness, and then the old professor, a soft-shouldered figure entombed in a too-large shirt. Still he thought he was one of them. You could see how he wanted to be liked, wanted to belong, and it twisted her heart. He praised the overt stuff, the girls' poems about their eating disorders, the boys' poems about what golf had taught them. She was the one student he didn't try to court, with her blocky fairy-tale-like things. They weren't really poems, they were stories, he said, stories that thus far remained unrealized. She didn't believe in labels, she said. It's not a label, he said, and she said, genres then, she didn't believe in them. Wilson shook his head, and she continued writing about small children whose fathers had missing hands or missing feet, or whose tongues had been cut out and replaced with internal organs. Pretentious, yes, but certainly less boring than her classmates' stuff. He worked her submissions over so meanly the class coalesced behind her. They anointed her the best writer in the group because she attracted the professor's disparagement. She challenges him, she heard the most beautiful of her classmates, a girl named Tandy Font, say.

He had food stains on his shirts, crooked glasses, a shy person's way of blurting out strong opinions.

She decided to pursue him when he refused to change her grade. As she stood in his office, fuming, she saw, suddenly, a change of expression come over his face, a little cloud of need, something so unidentifiable he probably mistook it himself as annoyance at her request. But the thought of this hostile person feeling something for her was so stirring that she decided right then and there, as he was telling her to take her quarrel to the department chair, that she'd be back.

She moved swiftly after she graduated, leaving notes in his mailbox in Hancock that she typed on a typewriter she'd found at a garage sale. The typewriter had a broken T key, which meant she could never say she *thought* anything, but only that she *supposed* he was lonely, and she found his loneliness lovely. The machine was a pain to use, and when he didn't comment on the notes' belabored nature, she switched to email. *You should know I'm not all uptight about sex,* she wrote. *I'm pretty unassuming about it. It's not this mystical thing.*

But that wasn't really what she wanted to say. *Honestly, I've only ever had one boyfriend before you. But it seems wrong to call you a boyfriend, somehow.*

When they were together he talked about art's power to narrate from the periphery, to subvert the expected, the sanctioned, and his words sort of washed over her like they had in class. He had a soporific, slushy voice. Something about him encouraged idle thoughts about his intimate life, the inside of his fridge, his frequency of masturbation. She knew she wasn't the only one who wondered such things—she remembered overhearing snippets of her classmates' conversations about him, though she'd never been at the center of them. She'd never been included at all.

People her age tended to avoid her. She had few acquaintances, fewer friends.

They consummated their union after just a few dates. Why wait? it seemed to her, and he agreed bashfully, then bucked and twisted over her and came quickly onto her stomach, a pooling like Cetaphil skin cleanser. She stroked his hairy back and felt her own litheness beneath him, her own fishlike body in his rumpled bed.

When she moved in with him, several of his neighbors asked if she was his daughter home from college. How embarrassed he was! Which told her that they knew nothing about him, that he was a loner, too.

They had her mother and brother over for dinner shortly after they were married. Stone Jay was three years younger than she, which made him twenty. He sold weed out of a little zipper bag that looked like a fanny pack for a bike. Wilson had cooked a chicken curry, and Stone Jay said he didn't like coconut milk and tipped his chair back on its two hind legs and surveyed Wilson's rice-serving and wine-pouring proprietarily. I'll take a glass, he said, and their mother didn't protest, so he had three. By the end of the evening he was playacting an intimacy with her they didn't share, slinging his arm around her shoulders and calling her sis.

He was always playacting something. He'd had a mixed martial arts phase. He'd tried selling solar-powered decorative fountains. He'd decided to become a pharmacist. He was so earnest about each endeavor, but behind the earnestness was a terrible duplicity, a trick he was playing on himself. His excitement felt shallow, dangerous. He said he wanted to be part of the clean energy movement. He said mixed martial arts was the sport of the future.

And the pharmacist thing? Well, he did have a lot of experience with drugs.

Audrey and Wilson used to argue about it at night—whether or not to help fund Stone Jay's flitting passions. She wanted to, though she would admit this only to Wilson. To Stone Jay she was stern, withholding, the public face of *no*. She knew he thought Wilson would've given him money were it not for his uptight wife. She didn't disabuse him of this notion. When Stone Jay's ideas fizzled, she felt guilty. If only they'd paid for him to take the prerequisites he needed to apply to a pharmacology program, she'd say, and Wilson would remind her that if something involved filling out paperwork or sitting still or drudgery or temperance or memorization or persistence or admitting to your own ignorance, that thing was not for Stone Jay.

After their mother moved into the assisted living home, he got a job doing landscaping there. Charges against him came almost immediately. He was stealing the residents' medications. He was eating the almond cookies left out by the coffee urns. He was sneaking into the cloakroom and riffling through the aides' jacket pockets, taking whatever he could get his hands on, their LA Fitness passes, grocery coupons, stray bills and change. When he swiped a box of their mother's microwave popcorn, their mother asked him to leave. He stayed away for a while after that, stayed away from everyone, the punching bag he'd hung in their garage as remonstratively still as a carcass. When he showed up again—maybe five months later—he had a shaved and badly nicked head and a case of pink eye. She asked him where he'd been, and he said with people who appreciated him.

You don't look appreciated, she said.

Looks can be deceiving, he replied.

The summer after high school Audrey worked as an usher at Monroe College's theater. There, she operated an old-fashioned elevator with a crank handle that she was forever stopping just shy of the second floor, requiring her able-bodied riders to take one big step up to get out, then pull their less-able-bodied companions after them. She could not get it to line up properly, because to do so she'd have to start the stopping before the stopping was needed, a reflex that proved unattainable. She escorted stragglers to their seats with a little flashlight if they arrived within five minutes of curtain time, and if they arrived after the five-minute mark, she didn't seat them until intermission. Occasionally, people she knew showed up with their families, and she felt herself sink into shame. But what could she do? She couldn't hide.

Or could she? The women's restroom adjoined a lavishly appointed lounge with a long, curve-backed sofa and frosted glass lamps, beveled mirrors and thick blue carpeting. She took to disappearing into the lounge after the play had begun, stretching out on the silky fabric of the sofa with a book. Turning pages under lamplight, she was peaceful, she was content. A bauble among baubles, lost to the dreaming rhythm of reading. The sound of applause told her when to return to her station. Some part of her recognized that this was what she should do for the rest of her life—that she should devote herself to books in some way—though she couldn't conceive of what the particular outlines of that sort of life would be. She knew it would contain her happiness. She also knew it would be impractical. With a brother like hers, she had to be practical, had to make up for him, if not externally then in the heave and whorl of her mind. Tidy thoughts, tidy life. But there in the lounge she could luxuriate, she could drift. One evening, a member of the theater's board of directors appeared in the lounge after the play had begun. She issued a warm greeting as Audrey scrambled to a sitting position. She was a pretty woman with dark hair and intelligent eyebrows, wearing a belted forest-green dress, and she betrayed no irritation, nothing but placidity, leaving Audrey to wonder whether she might understand, whether she herself might have read the book Audrey was reading (*The Beggar Maid* by Alice Munro), and might, even, sympathize. . . .

The next day, the woman called and fired her. She said the board had decided the usher would be a theater student from now on. It was hard to tell someone they were lying, but Audrey had.

Excuse me? the woman said.

I know you're firing me because I was reading. But I'd seated everyone. I would've heard if someone came in.

We're going to reserve the position for theater students, the woman repeated. It's very important. It's one of the most important positions there is.

So now you tell me how important I was? No one ever said that before.

She hung up, tears welling. She knew she would never be this kind of woman, who calmly and with surgical elegance separated the wheat from the chaff. Audrey was the chaff. She lay scattered.

She was leading someone—a single woman who'd recently gotten
a job at the college—through her Bonita Street listing. She had not
been inside the house since she was there with Wilson, and the rooms
still smelled faintly of bleach. The woman took in the fireplace, the
hanging closet doors, the O'Keefe & Merritt stove impassively. Finally
she shook her head and said, "There are no trees." Personally, Audrey
liked the overtness of the sun's reach, the house humming with the
possibility available only to that which was wholly seen. But she was
not in the business of persuasion. The woman would learn eventually.

STONE JAY

He ate from a bowl of flavored Tootsie Rolls while he waited in the lobby of his mother's assisted living home. Grape and lemon and vanilla—mutinous, off-kilter flavors. His mother was brought to him in a wheelchair. An aide parked the chair beside him and said, "Your mother is unsteady on her feet."

"It was just a little tumble," his mother said.

"She fell?" He pried Tootsie Roll from a molar with his tongue.

"In the shower." The aide patted his mother's shoulder. "Very common place for accidents!" she said, as if approving of her choice. "Very slippery!"

"I always told Audrey to make sure you were okay. I always said, you have to give Jay the help he wants, not the help he needs," his mother said.

"Well," he said, "it's Wilson this time."

"At least she's young enough to remarry." Residents shuffled past them toward the dining room, their massed white heads like a low-floating cloud. "And you?" she said. "Aren't there any girls you like?"

He tried to push her chair forward, but it was locked in place. Her body juddered. "Girls, or as they like to be called, women?"

He released the brake. "Sorry."

She craned her head around. "You're a handsome man!"

"Mom. Do you understand what happened?" he asked.

"Yes. Terrible."

"Wilson took his own life."

"You can't take it, you can only end it," she said irritably. "Other people still get to have it. They get to remember you however they like. Maybe they have you even more." She paused, and for one faint second he felt like bending his head to rest on hers. "Where are you staying? Do you have somewhere to stay?" she asked.

"With Audrey," he said.

"That's nice." Her knobby hands clasped each other. "Brother and sister, together again."

Staying but not residing there in any sense of the word. He returned to his mother's place, to the activities room, where there was always something to do, and sat with an old man and an old woman, ignoring the many empty tables available. He fancied himself an aid worker, bringing supplies to the hapless—his relative youth and cognitive sharpness—his pass to exit as he pleased.

"Do I have the right glasses on?" the man asked the woman concernedly. "Yes," she said, not looking up from her jigsaw puzzle. "What I'm trying to understand is, are these my distance glasses?" the man said. "You have the right glasses on," the woman said. She took a grim satisfaction in not affirming that he was wearing his distance glasses, that much was evident.

Made oddly self-conscious by the harshness of her voice, Stone Jay grasped the end of a brightly colored wooden stick, and removed it from its pile without allowing it to touch any of the others. He was clearly the most physically adroit person here. He removed another. The man questioned the woman about a Band-Aid that had come loose from the back of his hand. She was his remedy and jailor, his hope and doom.

His mother was wheeled into the room. The woman pushing her wheelchair walked with a limp. The chair moved forward then stopped, moved forward then stopped. He got up from the table and went to greet them.

It was the old woman from the canyon. She was wearing white sweatpants and white athletic socks with her American flag Birkenstocks.

"Meet Doreen Haskins," his mother said proudly. "Doreen, this is my son."

The old woman looked at him with a face devoid of recognition.

"Hello," he forced himself to say.

"Doreen's new," his mother said. "She's just settling in."

He saw her hands tighten around the wheelchair's rubber grips.

He went to the old woman's room under the pretense of helping her move something heavy. He could tell his mother was happy that he could be of some use. Maybe her son lifting a box onto a closet shelf for Doreen would cement their friendship, was what she was hoping.

Could she possibly not know who he was? He was both grateful and obscurely annoyed. Had she been traumatized so thoroughly? The wing she was installed in was newer than his mother's, its walls decorated with black-and-white photographs of baked goods—bulbous raisin buns, croissants with shiny flaking skin. Her room had an arched window that looked out onto a dry fountain surrounded by rose bushes.

"How are you adjusting?" he asked her.

"Oh, well enough," she said.

"You've got a limp, I noticed."

"You're a sharp one."

She wanted her bed moved closer to the window. "Is this okay?" She sat on the bed and bounced rigidly. "That's fine."

"Is it all right if I ask you what happened?" He turned to look out the window. He didn't want to see her face.

"I was shot. It pinged my hip bone."

"Who would do that?"

"A family friend."

He looked back at her. "Not much of a friend."

"You could say so."

"Is there anything else you need help with?"

"No. You're dismissed."

He returned to his mother's wing and rapped on her door. He had not been aware, as a child, of whether the house he grew up in was a pleasing space or simply a collection of chairs and beds and shoes and junk mail, but now, as he entered his mother's room, he was reminded of a quality that'd colored his childhood, an impermanence, a sense that there was no better place for his sweatshirt than the floor, because why bother hanging it up, or that it wasn't worth the effort to put the margarine back in the refrigerator or push his chair in at the table or clean the toilet or around the burners on the stove. It was everywhere—in oil splatters and unmade beds, toaster ovens whose crumbs smoked, broken strips of blinds. It was the desperate clutter of just getting by, the defeated arrangements of rooms in which nothing had been arranged. The refrigerator had to be wrenched open and farted out a smell of sour milk.

"There's more to Doreen than you know," he said.

She rolled herself back to her spot in front of the television and raised the volume with the remote.

"I'd hope so," she said.

He stayed away for a while after that. When he returned, it was to ask for money. His mother's aide intercepted him in the lobby. She said she wanted to tell him herself that his mother had moved in with Doreen. They still slept in their own beds, as far as she knew. They read aloud to each other from the newspaper, and Doreen wheeled his mother around everywhere she wanted to go. The aide had hoped she might learn to use a walker, but it seemed she'd lost her motivation to do so. Truth be told, it tickled even the most jaded eyes to see Doreen limping along behind his mother's wheelchair. They ate meals together and picked lint off each other's sweaters and debated the morality of social security. It wasn't romantic love, she didn't think, but the other kind, platonic. Was that the right word? Yeah, if it meant what she thought it meant, that they lived together like two old sisters. The aide regarded him evenly. Two old sisters who some-times went down on each other, he knew she was thinking.

His neck felt prickly. He had stolen lip balm from her jacket pocket once. For terminally chapped lips, the tube had read.

He turned around and walked back out the automatic doors and skirted the stucco wall until he reached the fountain. It was an un-usually clear day, the mountains' lines crisp against the blue sky. Er-rant set of shark teeth, carved-to-a-point rocks around the campfire of the valley.

He peered inside the old woman's window.

They were sitting together in bed, watching TV. When they saw him they raised their clasped hands to wave, like fighters after a bout.

He drank a great deal of beer at a picnic table with two men he met there. They drank silently, companionably, in agreement about what was needed. When they'd emptied the cans, one of the men jerked his head to the side and hocked up a loogie that landed at the tip of his shoe, a bit of blood at its center like an egg yolk's red freckle. Stone Jay stood and the sky reeled around him and he put his hand on the table to steady himself. "Next round's on you," the other man said. They had each other, while he was left to shuffle home like an invalid.

In Audrey's spare bedroom, he undressed and punched the wall. That night, he couldn't sleep because of his throbbing fist. He remembered how a man had come to the house once when he was very little. He'd come inside and wiped his feet on the doormat and then—this was the gesture Stone Jay remembered so vividly—reached back with one long leg and straightened the mat out. It was a rag rug, easily wrinkled. The care the man took with it struck Stone Jay like a revelation. The man followed his mother into the kitchen, and Stone Jay followed him. His mother said the man was an old friend and to leave them alone to talk. How is he? the man asked. Is he decently behaved?

The next morning he went to see a nurse at his mother's place. He'd sold a small amount of weed to her in the past. She handed him a flyer offering a $5,000 reward for the return of her lost cat, and he acted sufficiently concerned that she slipped him a Vicodin.

He entered the old woman's quarters without bothering to knock. His mother was watching her shuffle cards with a rapt expression. Lipstick wobbled over her mouth.

"I remembered something," he said. "Someone came to the house a long time ago, and he asked if I was well behaved. That was my father, wasn't it?"

The old woman knocked the two halves of the deck onto a card table.

"Why was I not more ambitious?" his mother said. "Why didn't I strive for more? A bigger life? What I wanted most was to be in my pajamas before dark."

"My father. Say it."

"I didn't know I had to demand his respect. I didn't know I had to fight him for it." She scratched the backs of her hands.

"How did you answer?"

"He said decently behaved, Jay, and I said yes. I agreed."

He felt suddenly blissfully free of pain.

"It did strike me that he'd come around like that."

The old woman began to deal. "What did he want?"

"I don't know," his mother said. "To gloat."

"What would he have to gloat about," the old woman said.

In his mother's closet, there remained of his father one blue sweater and a trumpet with sticky keys. There remained a handful of change in a bureau drawer. Why did it never get spent? He was just a kid. He wanted a Slurpee and a Skor bar. One day, when his mother was at work, he slid the large coins into his pocket and rode his bike to 7-Eleven. Casino tokens, the clerk said, pushing them back across the counter. Can't you tell they're not real? And yeah, they were a flaking orangey-gold and stamped with pirates' treasure chests, but he was bored, he was hungry. There remained a sense of deprivation. The only book he ever saw at home was the *I Hate Housework Handbook*. On its cover, a woman jabbed a mop at a child's drawing of a house, four lopsided windows and smoke curlicueing from a chimney. Occasionally his mother soaked hairbrushes in the bathroom sink. Occasionally she slid over the kitchen linoleum with paper towels under her feet. There remained a few stories, faint as vapor. His mother said his father had gotten her engagement ring out of a bubblegum machine at a horse track. She said he always bet on the horses with the names he liked best: *Grease Fire, Take This Job And Shove It, Twenty Licks*. She said he was hard to live with. His absence was everywhere and nowhere at once, like a dream remembered until the moment of waking. Stone Jay thought he and his father probably had a lot in common, but if he knew him, would he still think that?

ELENA

She got a call from someone who identified himself as Humberto Nuno Flores Muñoz from the American University of Human Services in Murrieta, who said he was looking for investment properties and had identified her as a motivated seller. She asked him how he had identified her as such, and he repeated what he'd just said in the manner of a collection agent repeating the amount of a debt. She said he wasn't answering the question, and he hung up on her. He hung up on her! It made her hands shake.

She went to find the boy and said it was fine for him to stay with her while Stone Jay was away but that she would need his help. She instructed him to follow her to Stone Jay's room, where she stripped the bed, told him to gather the towels that lay on the floor, and led him to the laundry room.

"I know how to do laundry," he said. But he didn't, really, she observed, as he dumped the detergent straight into the tank and stood flummoxed by all the buttons.

She enrolled him at the high school. The superintendent was an old friend, and a whole ream of paperwork was overlooked. An assistant principal gave them a tour. "We're gunning for the four Cs here," she said. "Connectivity, collaboration, creativity, and—shoot, I forget the fourth."

Impervious hallways thronged with students. Slamming locker doors like cymbal crashes. A meaty dishrag smell from the cafeteria.

When she pulled up out front at three o'clock, she came upon a group of boys gathered around him on the sidewalk. They were laughing. Someone was stomping on his knapsack. "Stop that," she cried out the car window. The boy got in. They were a rock propelled by a slingshot, there was that barreling commonplace violence to their trajectory. She drove to the grocery and bought chocolate milk and the ingredients for a simple supper. It thrilled her to buy chocolate milk, not just because it was something she would never buy for herself. He went back to school uncomplainingly. He never had homework. One afternoon she saw him soaking in the hottest of the springs with a copy of *The Old Man and the Sea* in his hand.

"This guy's in over his head," he said.

"The struggle's the point," she said, though she had not read it. Anyway, couldn't you use the word struggle about almost any novel? And reckoning? Dust jackets used those words as if they were so commonplace, as if often one struggled, often one reckoned, when really a person might struggle once, mightily, in his or her life.

Her superintendent friend called. "How's he getting along?"

"I think well."

"I've heard there've been some scraps?"

"Oh, really? I haven't."

He laughed. "I suppose that's natural. Keep an eye on him."

The time she ate the icing off a dozen cupcakes. The time she put small candles around her bath. The time she bought all new plates. The hope she invested in the inanimate. The time a man said to her, You have density, you have actual presence, how she realized later that what she'd taken as a compliment was a statement that meant *You exist*. The time she gave blood and fainted. The Dixie cup of ginger ale she sipped from afterward, feeling spiritual. The time she ordered a jar of expensive face cream that read *The best is yet to come*. The shame and thrill of reading it. The collapse of vanity. The puffiness at the backs of her knees. The time she went to the mall with her baby nephew strapped to her chest. How she let people believe he was hers, how it seemed people couldn't help but give advice to a woman with a baby strapped to her chest. The most common bit was to enjoy every minute because it would go by so quickly. The second most common bit was to let him get dirty sometimes. She went into A Pea in the Pod and bought a maternity shirt because it looked so comfortable. "You didn't wait long, did you?" the saleslady asked brightly, meaning, she supposed, the baby strapped to her chest and the one the saleslady assumed was brewing inside her, and Elena replied no, she'd actually never had a baby and wouldn't be having another, and maybe she sounded too pleased, too breezy, because the saleslady did not wrap her purchase with the pale-pink tissue paper she'd just tucked around another customer's, but dropped the naked shirt into a bag. The slight stung. She'd admired how the tissue paper frilled so beguilingly from the mouth of the other customer's bag. When she asked the saleslady why she didn't wrap hers, the saleslady replied that she didn't think she'd want her to.

She'd had to wear a back brace for a year when she was thirteen. The brace's molded white plastic was shaped like the bodice of a dress with a half-moon bite taken out under the left armpit. It was as hard and slick as a car hood. She determined not to let anyone see her in it.

She refused to change for gym class and was sent to the school nurse. *Bo Humphries*, the placard on the door read. When she turned the knob the office was empty. She paced the room, bumping into walls and pinging off them. A poster showed a rose bush festooned with every conceivable adolescent woe, depression and bulimia and obsessive compulsive disorder and self-mutilation and promiscuity and STDs, each bud a future bloom of pain. *Don't Stop to Smell These Roses!* it read. Another poster demonstrated how to properly wash one's hands.

She sat down, then curled into a fetal position on the tile floor. The room began to hum, and a fuzz of darkness filled her eyes, a tangled fibrous knot.

She woke to someone saying the same word over and over again in a gentle, insistent voice. It was just a sound at first, but it coalesced into something recognizable—into something shamefully intimate—while the person repeating it put his cool hands on her cheeks. Elena, he said tenderly. Elena. Did you eat lunch today? She couldn't remember. He helped her to a cot, where she picked quickly at her wedgie and smoothed out her shirt. He took her temperature and blood pressure and covered her with the softest of blankets, like a blanket on an airplane.

Now tell me if this has happened before, he said, pulling up a chair. Are you prone to fainting?

I don't think so, she said.

Feeling sad about something?

No.

Any trouble at home?

No.

Why don't you just rest, the man who must be Bo Humphries said, and left the room. She heard him give Tylenol to someone, and eye drops to someone else, and the drawer-scraping, feet-shuffling sounds comforted her, and her breathing grew slow and even. After a while he came back to the cot and sat down, sighed, flicked away the blanket, and gently slipped a finger beneath her brace near her belly button. He seemed to be searching for a hinge or closure, running his finger along the perimeter of it. It reminded her of when she picked her nose and knew she should stop but was determined to get at something in the back. She kept her eyes closed.

He went in another way, from the opening at her neck, swishing his finger back and forth over her squashed chest.

I can smell you, her mother said in the car on the way home.

Smell me? she said.

Something like fear or arousal's rising off you. You need to wear deodorant.

She kept devising reasons to go see Bo Humphries, and finally she was allowed to spend her PE period with him. She wore a silk undershirt under the brace, and they sat on mats on the floor and did stretches and easy, injured-person's calisthenics. She tried, and failed, to take deep breaths. Nothing thrilled and scared her more than hearing him say, Elena, now why don't you just rest. She assumed that thrill always carried a little fear with it.

He left the room, and she lay down, lay waiting for him to prove that she was human with a touch that neither one of them could acknowledge. He never did get the brace undone—it unclasped at the back. Later, when she came to understand the extent of the wrongness of what he'd done to her and searched for her outrage, she found a scratched melancholy, that was it.

Her mattress jiggled, and the click of a switch translated to something in her dream—she was in a doctor's office, a tongue depressor tapped against a glass jar—and punctured it at the same time, letting in light. She woke, squinted.

The boy was sitting next to her. In the reading lamp's brightness she noticed the bulge of his Adam's apple, the bone-edge of his chin. She was confused. "What are you doing?" she said. "How old are you, really?"

He paused. "Surprise," he said. He moved his hand along his leg. He was holding a gun.

"What's that? That's not real, is it?"

He blushed. "Of course it's real."

"That's ridiculous. I don't allow that here. You have to get rid of it."

"There's more in my room. Come on."

She got out of bed and followed him to his closet, watched as he removed containers of junk food and pallets of water.

"I've been stocking up at that school you've been sending me to," he said.

A dusty stuffed heart tumbled out with one of the pallets, something she'd purchased online from a site that sold anatomically correct stuffed organs. The site had said the heart would arrive with a name attached, and it did, *Travis Lumpp* stitched right onto it in looping script. It was the sort of rabid little thing she ordered when she was bored, and she'd never figured out what to do with it.

"You have to get rid of it," she said again, and left to go make coffee. Her phone buzzed. It was her second ex.

"I was going to leave a message," he said. "What are you doing up?"

"I could ask you the same."

"Thinking. Wondering why we don't approach this differently. There's no reason for us—"

"Do what you want with this place. I'm done here."

"What are you talking about? That's not how it works. You don't just walk away. For one thing, there are repairs, paperwork. For another, there are decisions—"

"Fuck you. Freeloader!" she cried. She hung up and smashed the face of her phone against the edge of the counter. A dense web of cracks glinted back at her, intricate and disordered, beautiful, in a way. Unabashed. She cleaned each room of the motel, scrubbed every surface to a shine. The boy washed the windows, leaving streaks. When she made out a rent check to her second ex, she wrote *I didn't mean it* on the memo line.

"Didn't mean what?" The boy was looking over her shoulder.

"What I said. Haven't you ever apologized to someone?" She put the check in an envelope. She turned off the pump that fed the springs, and there was a perfect moment of stillness when everything that had been obscured was audible again, the frayed voice of the traffic and palm fronds rattling in the wind and the sound of the air itself, which was like a distant room being thoroughly vacuumed, a carpeted room being prepared for a ceremony.

The boy stuffed clothes from the lost-and-found box into his knapsack. He tried on a pair of flip-flops. "Listen," he said, flapping their soles against his feet. "Bird wings."

When they left, she clipped the envelope to the mailbox. She'd forgotten to put a stamp on it.

THE MOTEL

The motel waited. The sun lay over the roof like an enamel lid. The springs evaporated and filled with debris. Hummingbirds darted from one bright thing to another. Soon the second ex would come and find the envelope. He would try to make sense of what she'd written, but he'd never been able to make sense of her. She had kept herself a little separate from him, though she'd have surely said she had no secrets. No one knew how others felt about them. If she'd known, maybe it would have been different. The beds were made, the ends tucked tight as gift-wrapped packages. He would lie down briefly and think of how they'd tried to have sex in all of the rooms. They had, hadn't they? Her breasts were like two puffs of air blown on a cold window. Clear for a moment in front of him. The rooms were clean. The rooms were ready. He would consider sleeping there that night but would return instead to his condo that had the Chinese character for prosperity on the door and a plastic cup of laundry quarters in the kitchen. There was nothing grand in his life, but it was familiar. It was a comfort that remained after everything flashy faded away. He would hesitate before putting the motel up for sale, but in the end he would.

THE BOY

They stopped at a barbershop on Twentynine Palms, where they got buzz cuts. "You in the military?" the barber asked, and Elena said she was shipping out soon. The black combs floated in their blue wombs. Their hair lay in shards at the base of their chairs. "Thank you for your service," the barber said as they left.

She drove much more slowly than he would have. "My grandmother used to say you have to survive not only what's taken from you but what you never had," he said.

"That sounds about right," she said.

"What have you never had?"

"Well, another life."

He felt his sense of optimism dim. For that was his answer too, what he was trying to find, where this trip was supposed to take them. But she had made it regular by saying so, and he felt he should have something else in mind. Her hands guided the wheel with minuscule jerks, back and forth, back and forth, as if she could barely take the strain of steering, yet they remained pointed straight ahead. The soft flesh of her upper arms shook.

They drove until they reached the canyon road, and he directed her to turn onto it. The sun was high. They were arriving like royalty in its strongest hour.

They cooled off in the river, then sat on the shore. Without her pink mop of hair, Elena looked uncovered, new, nearly pretty.

"You know I'm here willingly, don't you?" she said. "I'm not afraid of you."

"You should be."

"I'm sorry for you, actually."

It had been a dry winter. The river was low. Crumpled near them was what looked like a big black cape snagged by roots. He fished it out. It was the tarp, and he spread it flat to dry, and they slept on it. They ate the food he'd stockpiled, the chips and PowerBars and packaged cookies and dried fruit, and when they ran out of bottled water they drank straight from the river and got the runs. He liked going outdoors. It came quickly, recklessly, and he sprang away from it like a dog. A truck threaded its way through the brush, and they hid. A man in a straw hat worked clearing vegetation with a saw and Weedwacker. He stepped in something. "Shit," he said, angrily at first, and then, as he turned up his shoe to get a better look, "Ah, shit," gently, wonderingly. He made a call. "There's human leavings up here," he said.

Elena clapped one hand over her mouth and the other over his. He clutched her shoulders, and they shook in a paroxysm of laughter.

Their food ran low, and he slept later and later each day, rising and stumbling into the river, pushing through the measly current, drugged by sun and deprivation, the inside of his mouth sore, his nose blistered.

"You need something with vitamins in it," she said finally, and he could see what she was doing, appealing to his own interests, and he kept putting her off and putting her off until they were like animals, silent and suspicious, their eyes feral, their stubble coating their skulls.

She said, "It's time to leave," and he shook his head. "Don't say no to me," she said, and she wrestled him to the ground with surprising strength, and he felt her rolling hips and the banging of her breasts as she grabbed the car keys away from him. "Come on," she said, waiting for him to get up, and then she must have sensed what he was going to do, must've seen his hand inching toward the knapsack where it'd fallen in their tussle, because she took off running. He sat up, deflated. He waited, but she didn't return, and then he removed the gun and buried it under rocks and small boulders that he arranged in a pile. The power was in putting it down.

He heard voices and scrambled into a hollow that the trunks of two fallen trees made. A pair of hikers wondered about the rock pile's origins.

"You think it's like that place in Arizona with all the vortexes? Sedona, was it?" a woman asked.

"I never understood if the rocks stacked themselves," her hiking companion said. They posed for pictures and then scrambled around, cautioning each other to watch out for snakes. The woman fell and scraped her shin. She took a picture of it with her phone and then sat hunched over the screen, thumbs flitting about, no doubt broadcasting her encounter with gravity to her friends. Rock: 1, Human: 0. Other hikers came by, talking about their hiking boots. A couple narrowed down the list of names for their unborn child to a finalist that the mother-to-be worried wasn't definitive enough. For what did Angela really *mean*? she asked plaintively.

He half-expected his grandmother to be among them. He wouldn't put it past her. He thought of her shoehorning a shoe onto her foot, braiding her hair so tightly it shone. She'd developed a system of punishment and reward that she called good biscuit/bad biscuit. If he did something she liked he got a biscuit made from pancake mix, a pale square with pebbles of unstirred flour in it, but if he did something she didn't like he had to eat a dog biscuit, dry and dun-colored, or covered in a meat-flavored glaze.

There were other punishments. Licking the envelopes for her direct-mail business, three, maybe four hundred of them, until his tongue felt like stone, and then delivering them to houses and trailers on his bike. It was often cold and rainy, and he was pursued by rumbling flat-faced cars that peeled out from alleyways and under stands of dripping redwoods and sent him careening off the road onto the soupy shoulder. The sound of a metal mailbox lid clanging shut was the most forlorn, finite sound in the world.

It was on one of those runs that he found a puppy chained to a metal laundry pole, standing in the mud with no food or water. He unlatched the collar and placed the puppy gently in his bag and biked home with him nestled in the small of his back.

He gave the puppy to his school friend, Fisher. There was no possibility of being able to keep him. On the rare occasion that he went to Fisher's house, he held him and kissed him, buried him deep in his chest. But it was no good—the dog was Fisher's now. Its loyalty was perfect. It had one straight and one flopped-forward ear. Why wouldn't she let you keep him? Fisher asked more than once, trying, he could tell, to ask something else, like, Why do you never invite me over? Why have I never seen your grandmother picking you up from school? Why do you get that guilty look on your face when we go through my kitchen cupboards? Why do you eat so fast?

She just wouldn't, he answered, letting the exasperation in his voice be heard, and the pity. For he pitied Fisher his regular ways even as he envied him.

After one of his visits to his friend's house, he smuggled a photo album of Fisher's family home in his backpack. The thick pages were covered with something like Saran Wrap, and lined up beneath were images of Christmas trees and towers of presents, tables covered with plates of sugar cookies and candlesticks encircled by holly. The smiles of people used to having their pictures taken, unselfconscious, routine. Bright things in the background—paintings, pillows. In one shot there was a dangling wire basket filled with fruit, the bananas beautifully, ludicrously yellow. In another, shiny strung-together letters that spelled out *Happy Birthday*, and Fisher's cheeks ballooned outward over a cake, kids from school crowded around. Not him.

Pity and envy—spiky, contradictory feelings—combined to form a secretiveness that bored bone-deep.

His cuffs flapped over his hands so that just his fingertips showed, his pant legs pooled at his feet. He received a gift of shoes from a teacher once, a pair of red Converse that his grandmother made him give back. You're not a charity case, she said. You're not anyone's case but mine.

I'm not a case at all, he thought stubbornly. And realized later being a case would've been fine if not for being hers.

They went to bed at the same time. His grandmother tied a length of string around his big toe and ran it from his bedroom through the bathroom and into her room, where she tied the other end to her finger. He couldn't untie it and attach it to something else because she was accustomed to its gentle bobbing and pulling through the night as he tossed and turned. Its stillness would've alerted her. So some small part of him remained awake even as he slept, like a thrown-back fish swimming in darkness.

That was how they lived. Falling-out toothbrush bristles, gummy crumbs of scratch-off lottery tickets. Fabric softener sheets.

Fruity Hoops, Nutty Nuggets, tubes of toothpaste that just read Toothpaste.

He turned sixteen in boys' size ten jeans, seventeen in a size eleven. His bones were like the tongs of a wind chime. Five foot three—he could be a jockey, a pool shark. Subterfuge, temporariness, these were his natural elements.

Hey, you got any plans for the weekend? a duo of girls might ask as they passed his locker, and he'd concentrate on the dial as if defusing a bomb.

They'd continue on, their friendliness fading. Is that mean? one would say to the other with a little thrill of hope in her voice.

Once a girl at the locker next to his opened her door to an avalanche of condoms and sticks of bubblegum. She turned red and he felt sorry for her but he laughed because he thought that was what he was supposed to do. She picked up a plump little square with Ultra Pleasure written on it and waggled it in the air. Do you even know what that's for? she said.

His senior year, he was voted prom king. It was an ironic vote, though there was genuine affection in it. He was a kind of mascot. That was the confusing part, to be liked and mocked at once. Insulting, that they thought he didn't know there were two sides to it.

Crowned on stage at the dance under a banner that read *Class of 2015*. The queen had long waves of maroon hair. A throb of dancing opened to consume him. He let it have him briefly. A strange rising, almost of panic, inside the dancing bodies. The girls lifted their arms to writhe, releasing a smell of crushed Smarties. From the ceiling they must've looked like a field of fast-forward blooming flowers.

He threw his crown into the air, and it was caught and thrown again, and a game grew out of it.

Later, he left the auditorium to calls for him to stay. His fear was he would grow fond of them.

He owed a fee for a library book, so while he walked at graduation, he never did get his diploma mailed to him. It didn't matter, anyway. His grandmother's business went bust, and they headed south toward the sun.

Now he was in hiding. She had prepared him for this. It was woven into their poverty, their provisionary choices. It was why she hadn't wanted him to make friends. It was why she scoffed at the very act of curiosity. It was why nothing needed to fit.

If the world was corrupt, this was all you could honorably do. Crouch in a hollow. Be wary. Watch out for yourself.

(But wasn't it true, didn't it follow that if you had friends or family—help of any kind—you were likelier to be okay when misfortune came?

How would she answer that? She wouldn't. She never thought she owed anyone an explanation.

Never. She was poker-faced. She gave nothing away.)

The trees' bark was soft as cardboard, musty with rot. The pattern was like wet snakeskin, its grooves a gilled brown and gray and green. Dank inside, wetly enclosed, little mushrooms with long thin stems and rubbery caps growing in clusters at the back. He nibbled on one to find out if they were edible. It tasted of dark roots and cement and cheese powder.

He had to remind himself of what he'd done. That he'd chosen a stranger over the only person who'd ever known him.

A fever pinned him to sleep, a sticky sleep from which he could rouse himself only for a few seconds at a time. He'd come to just long enough to know he was going back under again.

His body was heavy with heat and then buzzing upward, alight with chills.

Finally he woke desperate for water. He crawled out of the hollow and looked around and headed in the direction he hoped was the river, stumbling forward and falling to his knees and continuing that way, tentatively, laboriously.

He heard it before he saw it, a whispering like rain. It couldn't be far. If he just kept moving he was sure he'd find it and find his grandmother there, washing her hair, crouching with her head to the side and suds in her ears and the strands caught up by the current. . . .

THE GUN

It couldn't help what it was. It was not the one to say right or wrong, yes or no, aim here or there. It was not the one to use itself. It had no grudges or anger or need, only purpose it couldn't interpret. The hands that held it were as unknown, as clumsy as wind-tumbled leaves. It was made of steel or aluminum or plastic, it was long or short, there was sometimes a little mother-of-pearl on the handle. It had a small black gaze that fixed upon its subject a small black eye. The gun was the gun in the light. The gun was the gun in the dark. The sun and moon moved high above its head. The beauty of the world, the precision of its passing.

TWO

THE GRAND-MOTHER

She came to beneath a blue nylon sky smattered with bird shit like the innards of cracked eggs.

It was very hot. She tried to sit up but pain bored into her hip. There was a weight, a smothering layer pulled over her legs and torso that crinkled when she moved.

Existence was really something, wasn't it? It called to you, and you strained to answer no matter how faint the sound.

She tried again, heaving aside whatever it was that covered her. The tarp, which released the blood-sweet smell of herself into the tent. She pushed headfirst through the flap into a stuttering brightness, a flashbulb going off and off.

She had grown up in the dark. Sometimes a glow came off the snow, like a pelt in the dim of a closet. The snow had been alive, falling and falling to earth, filling the swift distance it fell through with its own body, and it went on emoting even after it landed.

When she married she moved from Vermont to California for her husband's work. The fatal question came after the fact: what next?

She checked to see if she was bleeding. The wound was raw but not deep. She got to her feet and crept, bent nearly double, to the river and waded in. She didn't understand what had come over the boy, who had always followed her rules, who had never protested, or not much. They had lived under the same roof all these years. The way they lived, there was no room for trouble.

Only once had she gotten a call—from the principal of his elementary school, who said he was eating other children's food. Not demanding it. Not what you could call bullying, but coaxing, persuading, pleading.

She had not responded as the principal had hoped. Evidence of the boy's need embarrassed her.

It was harder to get out of the river than it had been to get in. She tugged, panting, at the thick cords of roots and stumbled on. The car was gone. She'd suspected it might be but still it made her furious. She had raised him since he was a baby. He had slept in a cardboard box with a little pink blanket that belonged to his mother. But his mother had been a gentle baby, not prone to wailing. Only television static could shut him up.

Oh, she remembered the feeling of freedom after he shut up. As if a deal had been struck.

And it had been, she thought. For the silence would lengthen unnaturally, and she'd tip-toe to him and place her hand on his chest to make sure he was still breathing, and there she'd feel the faintest up and down, like a lapping of water lived inside him. She'd stay that way for some time.

Now look at the turn of events. Look how he'd left her. She could feel that she was beginning to bleed again, a sticky, sappy creeping.

Somehow she made it to the road, where she waited a long time, waves of nausea and loneliness twining through her.

Finally, a truck driven by a city employee. She waved him down or he might not have stopped. "Can't you see I'm hurt?" she said.

He spread a towel over the backseat of the cab. "What happened?" he said, and then quickly, "You're gonna be fine," thinking no doubt of the trouble there'd be if someone died on him in his work truck.

She lay curled, hip throbbing. Each bump of the road sent pain jolting through her. "Talk to me, will you?" she said.

"Gotta be a hunred out here today. Gonna be a hunred at least for the next week." The man seemed to have nothing else to say.

She waited. "You're not very talkative," she murmured. She pulled weakly at the towel to bunch it against her hip. Her eyelids fluttered shut, but the light went through them. The light was a glaring, solitary figure with a headful of nails. . . .

A hospital stay, then a convalescence in an assisted living facility with a rehab wing. Memory Fountains—if that didn't bring to mind a specific image, nor did it ruffle the senses. Her friendship with Claris came quickly, unbidden, and they spent hours together as sun fell through the windows and wheeled carts clattered down the hallway and the strangely decorous odor of decay wafted through the air.

Though she chafed against confinement she found that she liked her room, which was light-filled and large enough for two. Claris stayed with her often, and eventually they requested a second bed be brought in. Claris had a hard time turning doorknobs and pulling up her socks. She had a hard time holding a toothbrush. Her hair was like a white rubber swim cap dotted with decorative flowers. She didn't particularly know what was what, that was the nicest way to put it. She had honed no defenses against the blobby vapidity of passing days.

The grandmother enjoyed being with her. It was like being with someone who had to be allowed to win at games. It tested the grandmother's generosity, her patience. Meeting the son tested some other part of her. The cowardly spawn. She pretended she didn't know him, or she'd have had to describe to Claris what he'd done. And then how would they go on?

Her wound healed nicely, but she was stuck with a limp. "What happened?" the doctor in the emergency room had asked.

"It was an accident," she said.

"You shot yourself?"

"My grandson did."

There was a second of shocked silence before he spoke again. Doctors were good at recovering.

But it stayed with her. That her own flesh and blood had tried to harm her.

The bullet had only grazed her hip. Maybe his hand was shaking. Maybe he had bad aim. Had he never fired the gun before? She'd had it his whole life, stowed in her bureau drawer. She'd felt no need to lock it up. What good was it locked up?

He'd acted erratically, thoughtlessly. He hadn't planned on doing it.

To consider otherwise was to slash open the sky and stand in its downpour, to let every dark thought fall on her.

Shady Acres Trailer Park. Eureka, CA. Chainsaw sculptures of bears and eagles and AK-47s stood for sale in front of the manager's office. The grandmother watched tourists run through the mist from their rental cars, gloomy, gloomy, this wasn't the California they'd bargained for but they wanted a howling coyote, they wanted an eagle with serrated wings. She knew what they wanted. She knew most things. She knew the bag boys at the grocery store would probably rape her if they got the chance. She knew that her daughter never should've married the man she did, who had tried to register the grandmother for the Green Party. The Earth was in danger, but he damn sure wasn't the one to fix it.

Knowing so much made her rigid with vigilance. She missed the days when she used to go to the Rotary Club with Betsy and Eleanor, where they danced with old men who shuffled around them like zombies traversing a house of mirrors, and convened between songs for vodka tonics. Spirits were high. The music was live. Eleanor wore her granddaughter's maroon Mary Jane–style Doc Martens, and Betsy wore a lot of rouge. The grandmother hated getting all gussied up, but she did weave a grosgrain ribbon into her braid. The good times ended when Eleanor moved to Ohio and Betsy married again and her new husband wouldn't let her go anywhere. He was a retired logger skeptical of friendships among women, skeptical of their need to get together and, as he put it, moan and gab, and eventually Betsy told her that if they met each other on the street of course they'd be friendly, but she had other priorities now. This she relayed in a prissy voice that caused the grandmother's heart to quake. Rain wet the sills. Rain wet the sills. The only thing that kept her going was knowing how much her grandson didn't know, and how if she wasn't careful he'd become just another sleepwalker blind to the dangers of being awake.

She used to do her deliveries herself, early in the morning, her head-lights catching the houses and small trailers in their last minutes of sleep, the best sleep, the most secretive. When the boy took the route—when she gave it to him—she was mostly glad to not have to get up so early anymore, but she did miss it sometimes. The quietness like the face of a clock. The houses were the numbers and the thuds of the mailers the ticking.

She wore stirrup pants and denim shirts and her hair in a long tight braid. Red dots—cherry angiomas—flecked her face and neck. She belonged to no political party, trusted no government, no orthodoxy. Stealthy individualism, maybe. It amazed her, what other people did out in the open, out loud, their lives like carcasses laid on a table to be prodded and poked, sliced into, examined. The shining bones, the tendons like ribbons.

She was not without sentiment—the opening bars of Fleetwood Mac's "Landslide," commercials showing young people getting loans at banks, commercials with dogs fetching their own leashes—as there could be nothing sacred otherwise. For even though the young people were not her young people and the dogs were not her dogs, she felt their hope and obedience keenly.

In the mailers were coupons for foot lotion and elbow lotion, turmeric supplements and toe separators, ginger scrubs and vinegar cleansers. *Treat Yourself to a Whole Body Experience*, the top page read, a prospect she found foreboding. To be touched was to be known, to be known to be found out, to be found out to be imprisoned in the minds of others. But there were people willing to try anything once. Or more than once, telling themselves they needed to give it time for the elixir to work, the troubled spot to be soothed, the hopeful act to bear fruit. People with theories, goals, exercise regimens. Faith in this or that berry. That her personal economy and so her well-being depended on other people's desire for well-being did not escape her. She offered them what she needed.

Their curiosity was different, insistent. The boy's teachers sent notes home with him about missing homework, missing lunch fees, that he'd worn the same shirt two weeks in a row. *Unclean aroma arises from student*, one teacher wrote, the note stamped with a smiley face.

Let them wonder, worry. It didn't bother her. The very best way to be—and this couldn't be bottled—was immune to what people thought. Immune even to their acts of kindness.

Do you think she loves the poor boy? she imagined them saying.

Of course the answer was yes.

She thought love was something you sat with, silently, full of the power of not showing it, of holding it close to your chest.

The boy was a Haskins because she made him a Haskins. Of course her daughter had given him her husband's name—Runyan—when he was born, which the grandmother could hardly fault her for because she had done the same damn thing, awarding her daughter, this body she'd labored over, this body brought forth from inside her by her own effort and no one else's, the name of *her* husband. The grandmother had kept her own name long before it was fashionable to do so, an imperfect rebellion, as Haskins came to her from her father. Men and their names were everywhere, drawing new lines and erasing others. But there was a beating in the blood that told you who you were, and she knew that was the closest she'd come. After her daughter and her daughter's husband died, she had Runyan changed to Haskins on the boy's birth certificate and shredded his social security card.

The boy never would've known if his other set of grandparents hadn't insisted on visiting. They'd steered clear when he was a baby— when she could've used the help—then came knocking after he'd reached school age. Randall Runyan was a recovering alcoholic. When he saw the boy's report card, arrived in that day's mail, he made a big stink about the name on it. (He didn't comment on all the Us for Unsatisfactory, the 1s out of 5.) To not have bestowed the name Runyan upon the boy dishonored the memory of their son, he argued. The son he referred to had wooed her daughter with his lofty ideals and aversion to the grind by spending his days tree-sitting, which he called his "real" work. For the grandmother to ask if this real work earned him a real paycheck was to betray that she was a capitalist shill. The pattern became established: her daughter's husband went off to protest lumber conglomerates and clear-cutting, and her daughter stayed home and made black bean soup, and then, around lunchtime, brought the soup to him to be raised by a pulley up, up the redwood's trunk to his little platform. The soup had a lot of cumin in it. Body odor and feet and a generalized sense of the unclean—that was what the soup tasted like to the grandmother.

After the report card was discovered, Nancy Runyan tried to smooth things over. Runyan's your daddy's name, sweetie, she said to the boy. He loved you so much. You should've heard him on the phone the night you were born. Ecstatic.

He doesn't know what ecstatic means, the grandmother said.

Well, inform him, then, Randall Runyan said. Teach him something.

It means very, very happy, Nancy Runyan said.

Was *I* happy? the boy asked.

He doesn't know whether he was happy to be born! Randall Runyan thundered. My god! He isn't sure!

Do you remember your dad at all? Nancy Runyan asked. Anything?

The boy lowered his eyes as if thinking hard. When he looked back up he said, If you tell me I will.

He was little, six or seven. The grandmother guessed Nancy Runyan would've visited again, once a year and bearing gifts, but Randall Runyan thought better of it.

The truth about her daughter's husband was that he was a conformist. A sheep. *Yeah man* this, *yeah man* that. She knew an antiestablishment mindset when she met one, and her daughter's husband's was more like mildly stoned with a sprinkling of revolutionary fervor. She saw the knives of bureaucracy (driver's licenses, social security cards, vaccinations, state and federal taxes) poised above her; he saw a bunch of paperwork he didn't want to fill out. She qualified for assistance (SNAP, Medicaid) that she didn't take; he was forever scheming about how to milk the state. The idea was a horror to her, being indebted to some program that some politician in Washington, DC, had dreamed up. And was there ever a transaction that didn't go both ways? If she accepted something from somebody, how could it not become something she'd have to repay? No, thank you. Scrap it all and leave people alone, she had said more than once. That makes you an anarchist, her daughter had replied, her eyes and nose ring gleaming. She used to carry her daughter around on her hip. She could make a pitcher of Crystal Light, boil a hot dog with her like that. Now, of course, her daughter would have plenty to say against the lowly hot dog. The way she talked . . . why, the grandmother had overheard her asking her husband, in a teasing, playful voice, where the naked mousie was going to hide tonight, leaving her to arrive at a stark understanding of what the naked mousie was. His dog-eared copy of *Desert Solitaire* on the same table that'd held her daughter's girlhood books: *Little Women*, *Little House on the Prairie*, *The Witch of Blackbird Pond*.

In the morning, they'd crowd the kitchen. Her daughter's husband had been a compact man, but his sense of himself took up space. Is there actual milk somewhere? he'd ask. As if the powdered milk on the counter was a decoy.

It kept her up at night, remembering his presumption. It ransacked the dark and let other thoughts in. You married to escape your parents. You married to escape the cold. You've been made to feel foolish your whole life. You want someone to treat you with a little respect for a change.

If only she could sleep through the night like her husband did, and leave the realizations to the banal light of day.

A van took residents of Memory Fountains to the mall and drugstore, the hairdresser and nail salon, and she accompanied Claris on her errands to get knee-high hose and chewable vitamins and have her hair done. She surveyed the streets from inside the van to test her equanimity. Did she want to be on the outside or the inside? Claris said her clavicles ached. The inside, she decided, though with some sadness, for it was a relinquishment to fall in love. She wanted Claris to see the canyon, and she asked the driver if he could make a detour. The driver was game, and though the other passengers were unenthused, they didn't protest. One of them murmured shyly that she did need to get back to take her blood pressure medication sooner rather than later. The van climbed the canyon road. It was beautiful there, like a well-healed scar.

"See?" she said to Claris.

The trees had so much light behind them they looked like ghosts caught on camera. The van pulled into a turnaround and sat idling.

Her thoughts strayed to the day, long ago, when the boy had joined some children in a game where they pretended to be shopkeepers selling sweets. From under a slide they offered cookies and cakes and pies to parents who rubbed their stomachs and smacked their lips after taking big bites of air, parents who lined up to buy more, rattling pretend coins in their pockets. The game went on and on that way until she approached to tell the boy it was time to go. He asked if she'd like to buy a strawberry ice cream, and she replied that she would not, because how could she be sure it wasn't poisoned.

Afterward she had wondered why ice cream, why strawberry, how his little brain worked.

She remembered seeing him naked. She remembered seeing him in too-large clothes. She remembered seeing him try to arrange his hair with a wet comb. They had lived in the beforeland, before the traps of diversion were set. She instructed the driver to drive on, feeling something crumble inside her, a rage that had positioned her in opposition to everything for so long that she knew no other way. To not believe in institutions was to reserve yourself as your own sanctuary, but what if you realized you'd given no shelter? What if you realized that not believing was a way to hold the burden of optimism at bay? The van rumbled along. Finally it arrived home again (did she mean home, did she think it?), passing bushes that had been clipped to spell MEMORY FOUT. It came to a stop, and she disembarked in a haze.

Back in their room, Claris said why not take a hot bath and the grandmother swatted at her and Claris grabbed her by the wrists. She seized the moment, Claris did, relaying to her several stern facts, namely that the grandmother would be quiet for a change, and would try to view the world through a less critical lens, and that fewer objections would be tolerated. Also they were to wear matching outfits from now on so they would never lose each other in a crowd. The grandmother moaned. Where had everyone gone? The boy, her friends, her daughter, her husband, who'd had a heart attack over a bowl of frankfurters and beans that she did not witness from her position in the kitchen, continuing to talk to him and saying his name sharply—Ted! Ted!—when he didn't answer. To have missed this moment of his, to have lived with him for over thirty years and have this happen when she was around the corner getting a second helping, was . . . the word that came to mind was unfair. She had seen so much, and his heart attack was the last thing to see, the end of a long line, the gesture that would both obliterate and explain. Explain how Ted had felt! He'd worked for a company that manufactured typewriters and then word processors. He'd been short with her since the day they married, but after his death she missed him terribly, and told herself he'd tolerated more than she had any right to expect. How she longed to see him again, to understand her limitations by virtue of his presence—what he would allow, what he wouldn't. The bully gives his victim shape. She went to bed and burrowed under the covers, and Ted was on his side of the bed again dreaming his own dreams, his head filled with visions of girls who weren't her, and she was free to do the same but his body was the only one she'd ever known, his furry chest and crenellated balls like miniature brains, and this was the room they woke up in, together yet apart, this was that room. It could be no other.

The day she got married, she had a terrible sore throat. She gargled with saltwater, and the ceremony went on. The band played covers by The Mamas and the Papas, and she and Ted moved to California the next day. The move was their honeymoon, she supposed, though they never referred to it that way.

They stayed in pine-walled rooms in motels on back roads. She loved the scratchy wool blankets of anonymous places, the lumpy beds, how the cold air clamored at the windows.

She made the first move because she sensed he needed her to. Once she did, a dam was breached. He put his penis between her breasts, between her thighs, wherever there was a little softness. Afterward, he lay on his back, snoring. She slipped into the bathroom. Her face and neck were rubbed red from his stubble, her nipples bitten and gluey. She reached her hand beneath the band of her underwear. It was like winding a wind-up toy, waiting for the flip. But she couldn't stand to see herself, mute and gawking, so she turned away from the mirror.

In the car, she spread the big map out over her lap and considered what route they should take. Yes, he had a job waiting for him in Eureka, but Eureka wasn't the California of palm trees and indolent beaches; Eureka wasn't even warm. Maybe they should veer off, head to Arizona or Mexico, someplace where the sun was high and hot and no one was expecting them.

She was nibbling on a cracker. You're eating like a squirrel, he said.

Cows, fields flashed by. She focused on one brown-and-white cow, its placid unsuspecting face, and thought that she'd never see it again, and the sadness of travel came to her. They drove through rainstorms, in one end and out the other. The dry asphalt on the far side looked puzzled, blank.

He never would stop when she said she needed to use the bathroom.

The word husband. The word wife. One a hush, the other a knife. Their sounds belied the power they signified. Meals in diners and meals in restaurants. Apple fritters, weak coffee, him sitting across the booth reading a newspaper that'd been left on the table. A buttery crumb at the lower left corner of his mouth. She let it sit there.

The coast was the end of the animal's body. Gray-furred, wild.

They couldn't see it from here, but in ten or fifteen minutes they'd be able to.

Betsy had tried to reconcile with her. In a letter, after her retired logger husband died. She could've come to see her, but she wrote a letter instead. *Dear Doreen, Dick passed away three months ago. Let me tell you why I listened to him. I was bred for obedience. Sad to say it's what I know. I'm sure we can be friends again. Love, Betsy.* A more honest accounting she couldn't conceive. Still, she chose not to reply. She knew it wouldn't be the same this time, without Eleanor, with the specter of Betsy's rejection haunting them. She would be bitter, ask too many questions, risk rejection again. An absent friend of perfect loyalty was better than a present friend of imperfect affection. She kept the letter folded in her bureau drawer and brought it out sometimes to reread it.

The grandmother and Claris attended a mock wedding for a couple of love-struck residents. The activities room was decorated with streamers and crepe paper bells that unfolded like accordions. A barbershop quartet hummed the "Wedding March" as the couple came down the aisle between rows of folding chairs. Hank wobbled, and Deepa steadied him with a hand on his elbow and a loving chastisement. Women became mothers again in old age. The pair turned to face each other, and Deepa straightened his tie and spat on her hand and slicked back a strand of his hair. That he still had hair made him a catch. They exchanged vows and kissed, and the grandmother was moved by their hopefulness. Afterward, there was a sheet cake with glazed strawberries and pink gel that spelled *Never Too Late for Love*. The first pieces that were cut made it read, briefly, *Too Late for Love*. A bride and groom figurine stood valiantly in the middle. She was waylaid by a memory of a series of porcelain figurines she'd received as gifts when she was a girl, one for each her birthdays. The figurines were blonde (she had been brunette), wearing long dresses with frothy hems and waist sashes and holding in their hands cakes upon which a shiny number 8, then 9, then 10 stood. Their noses were pert, and their placidity fatiguing. The whirling nothingness in those little heads! She could only imagine they meant something to her mother, who watched closely, hovering behind her with a laden patience as she lined them up in a glass curio case in her bedroom. Now someone wrapped the bride and groom in paper towels to keep them safe from the thronging at the cake. She selected a corner piece and left the room, the pleasure of anticipated solitude quickening her footsteps. Claris would be occupied at the reception for at least another hour. She enjoyed parties, and the grandmother didn't hold it against her, though parties made her uneasy. Parties made her downright querulous. She changed into pajama bottoms and sank into the recliner and took a big bite of cake. Sugar rushed through her, livening her heart. She ate the rest of the piece very quickly and sprang from the chair—she wanted to dance! Out of her pajamas and into slacks. A quick tidying up at the mirror, a rebraiding of her hair. She returned to the reception to search for Claris and found her talking to a man who wore a thick putty-colored hearing aid and clip-on sunglasses. White hair hissed from his ears. The man was describing a riding lawn mower he'd once had. He described it in great detail. He'd called it Rutherford B. Hayes, he said, and it'd never disappointed him. She waited for Claris to introduce her, or make some gesture that indicated she realized the grandmother was standing right there, but Claris did not. Claris appeared rapt. The man kept on. The grass had grown so green in those days, he said, not like today.

She squirted toothpaste onto Claris's toothbrush. She turned the faucet on.

If they ever had a mock wedding, Claris said through a mouthful of foam, they would wear white tuxedos. No more party dresses.

In bed, she pulled the neck of the grandmother's nightshirt down. Her hair dusted the grandmother's chest. Lower, lower, she thought desperately, but Claris hovered with demented fascination over her empty breasts. She tried to relax and enjoy herself, but her mind rattled with realizations—all she'd missed, all the unspoken rituals of tenderness, how one person could truly want to give pleasure to another person in a way that implied receiving by giving, receiving pleasure themselves by virtue of bestowing it. When she and her husband had ministered to each other it was always with the understanding that they were taking turns, her to him, him to her. The arrangement had suited her.

The next morning she said, "I never wanted to be married even once."

Claris replied, "A mock wedding, remember."

"Do you believe that outliving your husband is a kind of payback for all the time he took?"

"My husband left me very early on."

"But if he hadn't."

"I suppose," Claris said.

She didn't know how else to make her point. It would be another shackling, mock or not.

She didn't believe in marriage. She didn't believe in social security or Medicare (despite those programs paying for her convalescence). She didn't believe in taking people's guns away, despite . . . well, the gun had belonged to her father, the only thing he ever gave her, and it was, like him, stubby and powerful and mean. A burning at her hip, a sting in a sea of blank sound, the bang floating away. Despite, despite. Her grandson's face looming over her. And Claris's son's, rubbery and elongated. It made her laugh to listen to politicians so earnestly ask, Why do they act against their own best interests? The *they* was telling. *They* was so far from *we*. It wasn't interests, it was beliefs. She'd decided for herself what she believed, no one needed to tell her. She didn't believe in fluoridated water. She didn't believe in vaccines. She didn't believe in the PTA or the EPA or the DMV. She didn't believe in going to the doctor except to the emergency room when there were no other options, and there usually were. A hot water bottle, ice in a dish towel. She didn't believe in state testing. She didn't believe in libraries or bookmobiles or vegetarianism or ballet. She didn't believe in hybrid or electric cars. Was she going to trust her life to a—to a tin can on wheels? She didn't believe in psychiatry or antidepressants or coddling. She didn't believe in power to the people. She'd seen how that turned out. All the nonbelieving hardened inside her like a new world of bones, gave her strength and agility and kept her company when there was no one else around. She didn't believe in loneliness. She believed in hiding it away.

She was most herself when listening to talk radio, where the conversations so often became combative. She took sides, leaned forward, argued back. Claris said it wasn't worth it to get all worked up, but she said it was the opposite, it wasn't worth it if stupidity didn't alarm you and righteousness rang no bells, and Claris was on the ground.

"Pray tell," the show's host said. "Who put the moves on whom?"

The discussion concerned an ill-fated affair between a notary and a postal carrier. The grandmother pulled the cord that signified emergency, and medical staff came and took Claris away. She had time either to kiss her or to adjust her wrap-around skirt that'd twisted open to expose her thigh, the flesh like melted and refrozen ice cream. She chose the latter, for she knew Claris was prideful about her appearance. The grandmother assumed she had only fainted.

The wife of the postal carrier called in. The host could engage with three or four people on different lines at the same time. He was like the conductor of a plaintive and simple song that, one by one, more instruments joined until it was a rushing, swirling chorus.

"Is there anything you want to say to your husband's lover?" he asked.

"Waste of breath," the wife of the postal carrier said.

"A strong statement. Wendy the notary, surely you have a response."

Wendy said she never meant for something as regular, as pleasantly civic as mail delivery to become tainted by misuse.

"Cable bill," the host said, "water bill, advertising circular, *him*. The beloved. In those *shorts*." The room darkened until only the glow of the numbers on the clock radio remained.

The discussion concerned reuniting childhood friends who hadn't spoken in thirty years because one of them put gum in the other's hair. The discussion concerned the relative level of upset caused by a local exterminating service called Abort-a-Bug. The discussion concerned spoiled children. The host had incredible stamina and insight. He managed to tease out the damaging particularities without ever seeming needy. His was the cool blind variety of curiosity. She listened late into the night.

The show was called *Choice Words with Harrison Larry*. It played live from nine to ten p.m. and in reruns until one a.m. The discussion concerned indoor vs. outdoor cats. A defender of songbirds called in and conversed at cross-purposes with a cat owner who let her two tabbies roam and had had, yes, to dispose of their prey and even put the flapping things out of their misery herself. She said the flutter of a wounded wing tore at her heart but did not change her belief in her cats' right to freedom, to which the defender of songbirds let out a half war-cry, half wail. The discussion concerned a woman in an iron lung who had composed a hip-hop opera. The discussion concerned an actress who hired a stage manager to slash a rival actress's face. She didn't go through with the plan. Harrison Larry asked her why not. "She got cancer, so she kind of put herself out of the running." The avarice of people! the grandmother thought. The discussion concerned the lost art of hitchhiking. Callers rued its disappearance, said that seeing some guy with his thumb stuck out at the side of the road reminded them of simpler times. Of course, they admitted, they would never stop for anyone themselves. It wasn't an issue of safety so much as intimacy. To have to make *conversation* . . .

The next caller said no woman should ever accept a ride with a strange man, not under any circumstances.

"Oh, but they're not as helpless as all that," Harrison Larry said. "Haven't you heard?"

"I'm trying to save lives," the caller said. "I'm much reformed but I recognize ill intent. It looks just like me or you. Don't kid yourself."

It was true that danger lay just beneath the surface of things. It was true that plain robes masked lion skins. She dialed in to say so but was struck with stage fright, arrested by Harrison Larry's breath on the other end of the line. Her thoughts roiled and then fled, leaving her floundering. "I'm a mean old lady set in my ways, and you've never changed my opinion about anything," she said. "I enjoy your show."

"Much obliged," he said.

"How do you find these people, these subjects?"

"They're everywhere. We're surrounded, you know. You only have to pay attention."

An idea she had long been espousing herself, yet it scared her to hear it from him.

"If you look carefully enough, you'll see the double life," he said.

She said she was not often interested in the first one.

He laughed. "Ah, but does anyone know you're talking to me?"

She said she was laid up just now.

"Exactly," Harrison Larry said.

If she forced herself to imagine what Harrison Larry looked like, he came to her wearing a short-sleeved button-up white shirt with a pilot's epaulets. But she preferred that he remain disembodied, his voice his only feature.

"I've got a joke for you," he said the next time she called. "There's a building with three floors. On the bottom floor is a pickle shop, on the middle floor is a paint shop, and on the top floor is a butcher shop. One day, the butcher has a terrible accident. He lops off his you-know-what, and it falls out the window, past the second floor through a spray of green paint, all the way to the bottom. The next day a customer comes in to the pickle shop with a complaint. Your pickles are usually so hard and long, the customer says, but this one's short and squishy."

He laughed hectically.

"You think this is funnier than I do," she said.

But later, at dinner, she considered warily the paper-thin slices of meat on her plate, the carrots so limp she could bend them in half without breaking them. Back in her room, she stood close to the television screen and watched the antic images that danced therein. Lights flashed and grand music played and a news anchor announced that a gun had been found by two children in a local canyon. Then the mother spoke forcefully to the camera about the danger the discovery had put her pumpkins in.

She understood that the pumpkins were not real, and the gun was not real, and the canyon was not real. Nothing was real but her life here, and the predicaments of other people were idle and terrifying. She paced her room, which still held Claris's things—her clothes and toiletries, the round cases of powder and sticky-domed deodorant and shy little tube of anti-itch cream. The darkness grew, and *Choice Words* began. The discussion concerned a man who turned his garage into a house of worship. The discussion concerned a man who turned his garage into a smoke shop.

The grandmother was not able to speak to Claris, the aide said, because Claris was resting.

"She's always resting," the grandmother said.

"Yes," the aide said.

"Of course, no one always rests."

"Can I get you something?"

"I want to speak to Claris."

"She's resting," the aide repeated.

"Why is she always resting?"

The strategy was one of base repetition. The strategy was to enforce the rules. She knew how this worked. Build a wall to keep curiosity out. Repeat the nonsensical until it made sense.

"I would rest too, if I were you," the aide said.

"But what if you were Claris?" the grandmother asked quickly, triumphantly.

"Well, I can't claim that."

"You're not making any sense, young lady."

The aide laughed. "Oh, I'm not so young anymore!"

"Then you should know better. Please tell me why I can't speak to Claris."

And the aide, as if her brief human blossoming had come at great expense, let her face fall back into an imperturbable mask. "She's resting," she said.

The grandmother would soon be moved to the advanced care wing. She would be given three new medications whose side effects could include incontinence, confusion, and heaving.

She called Harrison Larry in despair. "I'm a patriot. Look what they're doing to me."

"Wasn't it Thoreau who said, 'If a plant cannot live according to its nature, it dies; and so a man?'" he asked mildly.

She sank into her recliner. Her nature was a hedge maze she wandered, thinking sometimes she was in pursuit and other times being pursued. A brisk knock at the door, and before she had time to answer the aide was striding to her side, plucking the receiver from the grandmother's hand, holding it to her own ear.

"Hello?" she said sharply. "Who's there?" She listened for a minute, and then placed the receiver on the cradle. "Dreck," she said. "He flip-flopped his name, did you know that? His real name is Larry Harrison."

She smelled of the kind of bright perfume a child might buy for its mother.

"You didn't know that, did you now, Doreen?" The aide gave her a canny sidelong glance and reached down and cranked the bar that collapsed the recliner's footstool, and the grandmother was sprung forward like a jack-in-the-box. "I read an interview with him in the *Inland Empire Magazine*. He operates out of a condemned middle school in West Covina. He has no professional training, he said. So why should he get to sit there and question people like a king? Make presumptions? We should call in and question *him*, shouldn't we?"

"I'd sooner," the grandmother said, but she could not think what. "They say that about you." The aide laughed. "They say you don't go along easily."

She called again after the aide had gone, desperate to hear his voice, to explain, to apologize if necessary, but the only sound to come over the line was a thin, staticky crackle. "Can you hear me?" she asked. "Can you hear me?"

She was standing with the other residents, waiting to enter the dining room, surrounded by a low thrum of voices. *Catalina pro shop. The date of the luncheon. Summer-weight comforter.* The fragments wound and flipped about her like cursed fish, and now she had to decide whether to try to piece them together. Of course she would not ask them to explain themselves. Without Claris as her buffer she was even more an outlier, silent and suspect. Fine, fine, to float here undisturbed, to confirm every hunch she had about the idiocy of small talk. *Now she says she believes in humility.*

The aide sprang forth from a pucker in the crowd. "There you are," she exclaimed. The dining room doors opened, and the gathered began to drain toward them. "I have sad news, so I'll just come out with it. I won't beat around the bush or hem and haw. I respect you enough, Doreen, to tell you the truth. Claris is gone," the aide said. The grandmother felt her knees soften and lurch forward, but she managed to remain standing by virtue of desperate will.

"What do you mean?" she said carefully.

"I'm very sorry. I'm so very sorry. It was her time."

"Time? Do you think we have times? Do you think death is like a dinner bell?"

The aide's face was rife with sympathy and turpitude. "Claris had a stroke. Claris became unable—"

"Shut up!" she cried. "Shut up!"

The heads of stragglers turning as they made their way past, assessing and sly. Whenever anyone got bad news, this quick judgment from the others: would they act so foolishly? For who at their age could not guess what was coming? But what no one told you about old age was you never quite believed in it, even when it was happening to you, you hoped the aching might mean nothing, you excused the broken sleep and the look of your own face, you remembered, vividly remembered better days, so perhaps, the generous among them admitted, they would, they would act in just the same hideous, heartbroken way.

The aide made little shooing motions with her hands. "It's under control," she said to them. "Go on, enjoy your meal."

The grandmother spun around and marched into the dining room and sat by herself, staring into space, and when she looked down there was a cup of hot water and a tea bag on a saucer on the table in front of her, but she could not have said who put it there. The surreptitiousness alarmed her, and the thinness of what it offered—the comfort of hot water with a little blackberry flavor. She pushed it away.

This was the trouble with caring and being cared for. It made you vulnerable. It made you weak. Alone, your weapon was always at the ready, sharpened and waiting. Your weapon *was* aloneness. She wandered to the edge of the world, where the masses waited, their bodies colliding and combining, becoming monstrously inquisitive. The thing she feared the most? Sympathy. When she'd returned to Vermont for her mother's funeral she was surrounded by it. Her brother gave the remarks while she sat rigid in her seat, her legs bound in itchy tights, her feet crammed into patent leather flats as if she were a child again. And indeed she felt helpless before some stagnant adult ritual, helpless to convey the ballooning dissatisfaction and anguish inside her. It would not leave her, that feeling, but became crystallized into skepticism, judgment. Rage and paranoia.

When the world was out to get you, you embraced first the reason and then the lack thereof, the simmering danger at the edge of everything.

Her father had dictated that his wife's casket be open, even though he had died before her—he had left instructions for her funeral in his will. Oh, the rigorous stillness of that face! she'd thought as she stood beside it. Its terminal familiarity, its lines and hinges, the puppet's clasped mouth, the sprouting eyebrows.

One of the last things her mother had said to her was that she wanted to leave the earth with her dignity intact. Yet the grandmother was aware, as she stood by the casket, of a sense in herself and others of scarcely being able to look away.

Afterward people expected her to talk, to make conversation as if a reign hadn't ended, as if a gulf hadn't opened, as if she hadn't been cast free into the world.

They expected her to tell them about California. She didn't know what they meant, where that was, that she lived there. And then it came back to her, the details of her life, the sound of rain, the sound of the gas burner going under a pot of water, the appreciative chatter of the women on the shopping channel who sold vacuum cleaners and jewelry and sconces and velveteen throws and shower curtains and rings. Burred purr of a rubber band sliding onto a scroll of mailings, bang of the door closing behind her, rattle of a reluctant engine. She'd felt such a keen sense of displacement, it was as if she'd traveled through time. It was cold here, and though only four-thirty, already dark. This was all she had to say: that it was already dark. Look. It was dark, yet your body wanted it to be light, and how did you reconcile that? Life went on in the darkness, a fact the average Californian would never understand.

Scratch of polyester pants, and a voice rasped at her shoulder. "Tea not suit you, Doreen?"

She started violently. How deeply she'd sunk inside herself! She gripped the table and stood up, rising as if through layers of water, and started toward the dining room exit, leaving her tormentor behind. When she reached the double doors, she pushed bravely through and there she stood in the kitchen, clamor of pans and shirring of high-pressure faucets, smell of stroganoff. Two figures bustled by going in opposite directions. She envied them, the people who worked here and could go home at the end of the day, the people who completed these tasks and were free to leave. She should be one of them.

"Can you hear me?" she said.

Why didn't they answer? No one was straight with anyone anymore. It was all dithering gestures, nostalgia, a vague incompleteness. She had succumbed to it herself, these sojourns into her past that, by visiting, she never quite left.

"Can you hear me?" she said again.

They circled her cautiously.

Once they'd arrived in Eureka, her husband brought a typewriter home for her from work. An IBM Selectric II. They weren't manufactured there—her husband worked in sales—but they had models in the office, and he thought she'd like to see one.

See one. Not use one. Would the latter presume too much? Would it seem too forward, too hopeful? The typewriter sat on the dining room table for a week or two, charcoal-gray with shiny black keys. It made her nervous. Finally she turned it on and fed in the paper and wrote *Your Honor and Mother, We've settled down in a little two-bedroom house on the edge of town. It's painted yellow though it could use a new coat. I thought about you when I saw that. Ted is busy during the day and I am learning the law of the land. I haven't met many of the neighbors yet but I'll meet who there is to meet eventually. The main difference is produce is less expensive here and the trees are taller and the men's hair is longer, sometimes past the chin. How are things at home? Your daughter, Doreen.*

When she read over what she'd written she saw two mistakes: she'd typed *law* instead of *lay*, and she'd called where her parents lived *home*. She tried again, aiming for a more overt independence, an explorer's toughness and grit, but she caught, too, in this second attempt, words that were wrong or potentially wrong. Growing up there had always been those two things. She crumpled the sheets of paper and chucked them into the wastebasket, wishing she could address herself to her mother alone. She might say something about Ted then, something careful, like how did anybody really know what they wanted? How had her mother? To question was safer than to confess, for if her mother decided not to understand her, she could claim she was just curious, she hadn't meant anything by it. Her mother was an unreliable confidante, apt to play dumb. She went through three or four more drafts until she'd arrived at a letter of bland facts and impersonal details, and she folded it and put it in an envelope and addressed it to home even as she admonished herself not to think of it as home anymore, to think of it as a way station, a shack on a mountain with supplies for hikers, cold bars of soap and cots and moth-eaten bedding, maps with shaky red routes like spider veins. When Ted got home he took in the brimming wastebasket and then he said he'd heard the wastebasket was the author's best friend, so she must be turning into an author. A budding author, is that right? he said. Are you going to put me in your stories? I was just writing a letter to my parents, she said, a mistake to answer his teasing with fact, for it took too seriously his question, it justified it in some way. I was just, I was just, he mocked. Why don't you leave your parents alone and make me dinner.

Her pregnancy was hard at first—she spent days in bed, weak and sick, rising only to totter into the bathroom and kneel in front of the toilet and vomit, rinse out her mouth, fall back into bed. She tried to stave off the nausea that inevitably returned by closing her eyes and envisioning a pail of cold, clear water being hauled up from a well, tipped over, poured out. The sparkling threads, the quicksilver sheet of it like a curtain behind which some kindly figure stood. After her first trimester the nausea subsided, and she felt downright giddy during the second. Giddy at not having to beg Ted to pull the car over so she could throw up pale strands of spaghetti in a heap on the side of the road, which annoyed him, as if he thought a stronger person, a person more in control of herself, could've held off until they got home. It wasn't the immodesty of it that bothered him, she didn't think. If she had to say, she would say it was his having to wait for her. Afterward, he did not help her back to the car. She got in, buckled up, said okay. Weak but relieved. Wasn't it wonderful to have that over. Maybe she could try some ice cream when they got home.

Can you go two minutes without talking about food? he said.

She slept on her side and crept down the dark stairs to use the bathroom during the night. Later she realized how easily she could have fallen, but at the time she didn't think to keep a flashlight next to the bed. Such a simple solution. Maybe Ted wasn't aware of how often she took those treacherous stairs. She was sure he wasn't aware. He slept heavily, with no arm extended. He took the covers with him when he turned. In other marriages there existed a kind of tribal subjectivity that made the couple staunch defenders of each other, at least in the presence of others. With Ted she never knew who he might defend.

She thought their marriage was doomed to be prickly. She didn't believe it could be otherwise.

He was at work when she felt the first labor pains. She called him, and he told her to call a taxi, and she did, and at the hospital she was borne away by a knowledge of what she had to do—the instructions, the things they told you might or might not happen, meaningless. What was inside her hardened and turned, like a plastic flower toward the sun, and then she felt an urgent need to push.

Her labor lasted less than three hours. Ted arrived after their daughter was born.

He was at home when they got the call about the accident. Their daughter's husband had lost control of the car, a not-uncommon occurrence on the 101. A dark wet night. Marijuana cigarettes on the driver, on the passenger, in the glove box. Seatbelts off, radio on.

Dimly, she wondered what was playing. She imagined her daughter's hand going for the dial and her husband elbowing it away and the car crying out, crying like a train coming to a halt on a long, curved track. The song of metal . . .

Oh, he was a bastard! Yet she had given her daughter to him by not keeping her to herself, and now the baby was all there was.

The boy got home from doing the deliveries at half past seven. He had the sense to remove his shoes at the door. His soles were plastered with wet grass.

She had already set the table, and there was a Sara Lee pound cake waiting in the kitchen. She'd been defrosting it all day.

One twenty-two Linden Terrace is a duplex, but it doesn't look like it. There's a one twenty-four, she said as they ate.

I know, he said.

Don't talk with your mouth full.

He swallowed. She could see the slow lump sink down his throat.

Did you happen to notice if anyone's moved into that corner house on Alderman? she said.

Yep.

You did notice?

Yep.

And they did?

Yep.

So you delivered there?

He took a bite. Yep.

I can hear your teeth on your fork. It's a terrible sound.

She brought out pieces of pound cake with the cool golden crust. He looked at his indifferently, then got up from the table.

I'm not hungry, he said.

I don't care. I paid good money.

She watched him sit down and take a bite. Again that mouse-sized gulping. Don't you like it? she said. You don't like it?

It's fine, I guess.

Would being out on the street be fine with you too? Soggy and wet? She carried her plate to the living room and turned on the TV, where a stern voice pressed upon the public the toll-free number to call if they'd had botched lap band surgery, a demographic that surely would not let a Sara Lee pound cake go untouched.

He'd thrown his piece away, she saw later, looking in the trash. The hopeful, happy cake—ruined.

When she complained about it to Betsy and Eleanor, they said, Well, why would you make him eat dessert?

As if it wasn't obvious—that this—this was what families did.

She limped as quickly as she could past half-open doors, beyond which lay bodies like sticks of margarine on white plates. Something so still, almost preserved about them, as if a deep recognition of their fate had taken hold and further motion deemed unnecessary. Moaning drifted occasionally into the hallway like heat from a vent. In a room at the very end, a woman sat in a chair, notable for her uprightness. The bed had been stripped. A wilting bunch of get-well flowers sprouted from a vase, their petals falling luxuriantly, wantonly onto the end table.

It was Claris. She had color in her cheeks and fantastically black hair. The grandmother was so happy to see her. She went to her and grasped her hands. "Here you are, here you are. They said you'd gone," she exclaimed, unchagrined at her emotion.

Claris looked at her strangely but let her hold her hands.

"They wouldn't let me see you. They were unrelenting about it," she said. Claris began to cry.

"Now, what's that?" she scolded, though she understood, she did.

"Are you Doreen?" Claris said through her tears.

"Quiet, Claris. You shouldn't talk nonsense—what's it ever gotten you? You should approach things head on. I'll make you a cup of coffee when we get you home."

This elicited more jagged sobbing. The grandmother stayed mum until it subsided. It used to work with the boy, letting the squalls pass, letting the inchoate, severe cries run their course. She placed her hands on Claris's cheeks.

"Your hands are cold," Claris said softly.

"Warm them for me," the grandmother said.

Claris's face was incandescent. Her lashes were sparkling wet. There was something unfathomable about her, and the grandmother could see that what she'd mistaken for uncomplicatedness was really that she hid things so deep inside her they became ungraspable, like a rope frayed by time or wind. The two of them sat on the bed holding hands. Claris's pulse tapped strong and steady against her finger. The squiggly brown blotches on her cheeks were gone, the moles and marks of age. Her skin smelled marvelous, like cherry pie. When the aide came in, Claris gently untangled their hands and stood.

"Oh good, Audrey," the aide said. "I see you've met Doreen."

The aide was an idiot, the grandmother thought.

Her beloved cleared her throat.

With a few hushed words, she was able to make the aide leave them. "Let me tell you about my mother," she said.

Her mother had been a distant woman. A roving ghost who took a startlingly physical shape. Her mother wore sheepskin slippers with a woolen lining that bore the imprint of her feet. She, the daughter, hid them sometimes, feeling closer to those slippers than she ever did her mother, to the mute and true way they carried her shape, and her mother would make increasingly distraught circuits of the house looking for them under beds and in closets and, improbably, the bathtub, and she'd help her look. Her mother told her not to eat too much. Once she, the daughter, was at a friend's house, and she saw her friend and her friend's mother do a little sliding side-to-side dance—music was playing, her friend's mother was wearing bright white Keds and a loose blue dress—and she thought it was the most wondrous display of tenderness and ease she'd ever seen. Her friend's mother had made bread and served it warm with butter. The bread was honey-brown and knotty with oats and served in thick slices on pottery plates with a dripping, exuberant glaze. The house was filled with bright rugs bitten through to their threads and wooden African masks and jangly modern art and the jazz records her friend's father played. She thought of home, the linoleum floors, the sound of the weather report. This was a damning statement, but she was going to make it anyway: she'd never gotten what she needed, which was just a little beauty. A few decisions made in its service. An acknowledgment that life didn't have to be pieced together, slapdash, untidy. And yes, she knew it had to do with money, and that her friend's family had money and hers didn't. Still, things could've been made to look nice if her mother had wanted them to. Her mother had no appetite for the ineffable.

The grandmother felt an odd duty to defend the mother.

"But she talked about you, while she was here. She talked about nothing for years, not my father, who'd run off, not my brother, who was totally rootless, not my husband, who was my college professor, but she did talk about you. She said you forgave. And that became important to me, given what happened to my husband, or I guess I should say what my husband did. Every trauma is different, but you'd be surprised by how the path to recovery takes the same—"

Her cadence was the cadence of a far more verbose and self-satisfied person than Claris had ever been. This need to explain, nearly to boast.

"What about your children?" the grandmother asked.

She shook her head. "I don't have any."

The grandmother knew that was not true, that she had a daughter and a son. She knew the son was difficult, just as her own grandson had been. She had taken solace in that thought, that there had been a boy, and then a man too, for Claris, who had remained a separate entity, close in proximity but not in any other sense of the word, a symbol of something you'd rather forget, something that reminded you of what you'd lost and what you'd given up.

THREE

ELENA

The windshield was so dusty she could hardly see through it. The glare was granular, the high, hard ball of the sun filtered as if through orange mesh.

A voice on the radio was reading a story by Kate Chopin. "She did not stop to ask if it were or were not a monstrous joy that held her," the voice said. She listened as she drove, staying on surface roads, a loose, regaling light all around her. When she came to a building the color of wisteria, she pulled over.

She was somewhere in West Covina or El Monte, she thought. The towns bled into one another. She surveyed the stream of traffic she'd fallen out of, its pattern of moving, the spaces between the vehicles expanding and contracting like wooden beads on a wire. SUVs and big-bodied trucks stirred litter into clots that scudded across the street and jumped the curb. No one slowed for her. The drivers raced toward a perfect future, and she was a figment of an imperfect past, wind-tousled, sunburnt. She unfolded one of the clots to an advertisement for a descaling powder, something to be poured into coffee makers.

All the hectic energy of the road went out of her then. She turned and made her way toward the building.

Inside, an empty vending machine stood humming, its coils like the springs of an overturned mattress. She wandered past a bank of chewing gum–plugged water fountains down a long tiled hallway that opened onto rooms on both sides. The rooms had blackboards in them, and plastic desks and chairs stacked along the walls, and caged stopped clocks. At the end of the hallway, one door was closed.

A woman walked past her. "Are you from permits?" she asked.

She shook her head.

"Who're you here for?" the woman said. "Are you here for Harrison? Why didn't you say so?" She rapped on the door. "Harrison?" Her toes thick in their bejeweled flip-flops. She rapped again, jerked the handle back and forth. "Someone to see you," she called.

"Who's Harrison?" Elena said.

"All right," the woman called, "I'll show her out. I'll tell her you're inoperative. Quivering in a gelatinous ball. I'll tell her to come back later."

"Oh, I'm not—" she started.

The woman swung around. "Are you one of those gals who thinks it's about *you*?" She pounded on the door with the heel of her hand. "Harrison, we know you're hurting, sweetheart. Please open the door," she said.

Elena sank to the floor.

"Let us talk to you. Let us help. We can have a little chat and see if we can't figure out what's wrong. You're *wanted*, sweetheart, can't you see that? We *want* you terribly." The woman raised her eyebrows ironically. "I find that appealing to his vanity usually works," she said. "You know, I did love him once upon a time, very long ago. We rode horses in the canyons together. It was a great meeting of minds to see Harrison with a horse."

A wave of exhaustion came over Elena, who leaned her head against the wall and closed her eyes.

When she woke it was to a sense of rearranged air. The door had been opened. She got to her feet and peered inside. A man sat behind a console with horizontal rows of red and green buttons and vertical rows of sliding black knobs, a headset slung around his neck. Lank strands of graying hair escaped from his ponytail and were mired in his stubble. "Here I am," he said. He fiddled the knobs up and down. "Not much to see."

The unsolved equations on the blackboard in this room seemed indicative of a cosmic precariousness.

"You do a show here?" she said.

"Show is such a limiting word, but yes." He was wearing a ribbed white undershirt, fog patches of hair on his shoulders. "Are you a fan?"

"A fan," she repeated.

"Sit down. That's nice," he mused. "That's reassuring. It's been a while since anyone's said that. She used to have to turn them away." He jerked his head to indicate the door and the woman who'd been banging on it. "She used to be one herself. Yeah, she hung on to my words."

There was an apple sitting atop a filing cabinet, gleaming like a piece of plastic fruit. He handed it to her, and she tasted it before she got it to her mouth, its sour and inexact sweetness, and devoured it quickly to the core.

"Where've you been?" He opened a drawer in the cabinet and pulled out a sandwich. "It stays coolish in there."

Tuna salad. She ate it very quickly as well. She knew she should save a half for him but didn't.

A button on the console started blinking. He put on the headset and pressed it. "Choice Words with Harrison Larry. Yes. No. Of course. Of course. Of course. Your prerogative." He let the headphones dangle around his neck again, and the expression of self-regard on his face loosened into vagueness, then plaintiveness. "Creditors and bandits. Thieves. Soulless jackals in pointy-toed shoes. They don't understand what I do, they have no interest beyond numbers. Their brains are like toasters: put numbers in, wait for profit to pop up. In the meantime I'm illuminating the cave. You remember the discussion of how greed leads to evil and binds us to suffering? You remember the discussion of gifted organs? You know better than anyone."

"I don't, actually," she said.

He raised his eyebrows.

"I have no idea who you are."

"Why," he said, "you're an innocent." His eyes shifted focus, seemed to take her in more closely, his pupils like two black wafers. She blushed, and hoped she might stanch the blush's spread by regarding it with derision. A blush, give her a break. He thrust the headset at her, and she took it from him and put it on.

It had something of a sleep mask's claustrophobic softness. "Is anyone there?" she said.

"Of course someone's there. What you want to do"—it was warm, too, warm from him—"is greet them. Go ahead. They're there, no doubt about it. Don't broadcast your insecurity. They want your strength, the strength of your mind, and if they knew the squalor, the bitter taste of your"—he flung his arms out—"surroundings, it would undermine everything. Your reputation, your confidence and power. Deliberate questions only, probe even as you appear not to probe, climb down, down into the heart of the matter. Messy things, hearts, turbulent splotches of meat, really. I've gotten adept at reading them. I can see you're hurting. You think you can outrun it, start over again someplace else, but we're already in the kingdom. It's all gold here, all heat. I don't believe in anything but this state. I don't believe in myself beyond its borders. I went to Virginia and wanted to die, I wanted to shrivel up and disappear. I was there on a date. A beauty out of all proportion, her profile read, and it really did describe the abundance of her limbs and these long, heavily perfumed locks she had. She fed me grilled peaches and vanilla ice cream, but the place didn't agree with me, the land didn't. You know how I felt? Like the green was going to tangle me up in its tendrils, pull me over, swamp my bones. I returned to California as quickly as I could. It wasn't defeat. It was—"

But how do you know, she thought stubbornly even as he went on talking. This was her weakness, the sound of a voice that otherwise might not have anything to say to her unless she held still and listened.

FOUR

THE BOY

The manager of the trailer park kept gummy mints shaped like ever-green trees in a glass ashtray in the office. If he stopped by she'd give him one with only a bit of small talk required. The space heater blew against his knees, and the green mint sweated in his hand. He could feel the coarse grains of sugar pricking his palm, but he was waiting to leave to eat it. Did she think he was a nuisance? A poor lost sheep? A future malingerer, lowly and innocent and terrible and greedy for anything anyone might give him? Maybe she didn't have an opinion of him. Maybe he was only what she saw, a kid standing there warily, shifting from foot to foot. She asked about his grandmother, simple questions to set him at ease. She was a wry-faced woman with creaky joints—she complained about her aches—and a secret seriousness. He'd seen her when she thought he wasn't looking, wearing an expression that meant she was bothered by something. He replied that his grandmother was fine and that no, they didn't need anything, even though the trailer's window screens were ripped and the sills furred with mold. The carpeting was the fake-grass kind usually found on porches.

A radio played jazz at low volume. He liked how she listened to this jittery music so softly it bubbled into one strain, and thought it would be nice to do his homework there.

It would be nice to do his homework anywhere other than at home.

Once she kept him talking so long the mint turned to jelly in his hand, and he was confronted with a terrible choice: place it in his mouth and be seen eating it, or get rid of it. He snuck a glance—the mint glowed from the softness of his palm like a jewel on a velvet tray. Reluctantly, he loosened his fingers. He heard it hit the ground, stepped on it, and smudged it out.

She blinked quickly several times. You know, I could use some help hauling wood from my truck. Set up, clean up. I assume you don't mind a little sawdust. Would you be able to help me occasionally? I'd pay you, of course.

The question posed so casually, as if she weren't setting him up for a mad rattling of his cage. But because she was their neighbor, because they could see her trailer from theirs and smell when she cooked a hamburger on her grill, he mentioned her request to his grandmother, who was microwaving an orange pouch of queso sauce. She gave him a withering look and wheeled around and marched outside and came home later with an agitated, triumphant face.

What did you say to her? he asked desperately.

She spat into the sink. That you work for me, she said.

Later he plunged his hand into the sink for something and touched the gelatinous blot.

He continued to see the manager from a distance, in overalls and rubber boots, working on one sculpture or another, a roadster or a windmill or a lighthouse. Sometimes she waved. Sometimes he waved back. Then the day came when he realized he hadn't heard the whine of her chainsaw lately. It had been as habitual as birdcall, easy to ignore. The silence was a spreading, needling absence, louder in its own way. He was graduating in a few weeks and felt a burgeoning sense of freedom, and he went to the office on a whim. It was wood-paneled, with a counter you lifted to get to the back, where she kept a bulky desk and a calculator and a Churchill Downs calendar. It had been years since he'd been in the space, but nothing had changed.

Look who it is, she said when he entered. She got up from the desk and gestured toward the ashtray, which held paperclips now. You were the only one who liked them.

Her hand tremored. There was a light smattering of rain against the roof, the kind that portended a heavier downfall.

I was? he said.

You were. You relished them, but you were careful, wary of pleasing yourself. I wish I'd done more to try to pry you out. I wish I'd stopped *by*, you know, just to see what was what.

The rain roughened.

You were a kid. How could you have been expected to know that it wasn't your fault?

Now he wished he hadn't come. What wasn't?

She's a tough nut to crack, a notorious crank, if you don't mind me saying so. Intimidating. Confusing. So for a child to have to grapple with her moods, her ways, her suspicion and paranoia . . . well, I regret not doing more. There was one question to ask, damn it, and I didn't ask it. But the situation here—she gestured toward a disheveled stack of paperwork on the desk—the situation is that she just won't work with me on this. She's five months delinquent on rent. She hasn't responded to my notices, to my threats. It's out of my hands now. I've turned it over.

Don't. Don't bother her! he said.

It's out of my hands, she repeated.

I'll get it from her. How much does she owe?

It's too late, I'm afraid.

Please give me what she owes. I mean, tell me.

She wrote the sum on a piece of scrap paper, and he shoved it into his pocket. Walking back to the trailer, he thought about how last Christmas he'd ordered something for his grandmother from her coupon book, planning to keep it hidden in his closet and surprise her. He thought she might like something for herself for a change, a turquoise plastic footbath that plugged in and heated and swirled the water. He was gone when it was delivered. His grandmother confronted him with it.

What is this? she asked. Some useless trinket I sell to those people?

Some made-in-China dinged-up piece of trash? Her face was vehement, shuddering. You do understand that as a society we have a death wish? Buying our own destruction, wrapping it in pretty paper, giving it to each other as if it's a kindness. I regret the part I play in it, but on the other hand the market's the market. I'm surprised at you. Maybe I'm not. Maybe you always wanted to be one of them.

They stood regarding each other. His grandmother pushed the box into his chest, and his arms tightened around it. He would assemble an arsenal of their stuff. He would learn their language and customs, even if he was only a visitor. A visitor marked by his difference, by some shifty alternate origin that others could sense. He could practically hear them thinking that it wasn't his fault, but he made them uncomfortable nonetheless.

It was a mistake, he said.

A gift, she said. You've become so conventional.

Now he dipped his hand into his pocket and crumpled the piece of scrap paper into a pebble. The sum was thirty-four hundred dollars, but it might as well have been three million. She would never pay a debt; she would never stoop to do so. To pay a debt would be to lend credence to a system she didn't agree with, something orderly and hierarchical and anonymous, something that knew her but didn't allow her to know it. In its rigidity, in its remove, it had all the power. Leaving her with only the power of refusal.

They left Eureka not long after that. His grandmother instructed him to put his belongings in plastic garbage bags and heap them at the curb. In the car, she failed to fasten her seat belt. Rain ran sideways across the windshield. The old Victorians with their turrets and pitched roofs, the boardwalk, the dock, the water that brought with it a wet-wool chill, the crowded sky of clouds, the yellow windows in the morning dusk. They left it all behind. His grandmother took the 101 s-curves too quickly. The speedometer was broken, but he could see the hastening of the landscape, the trees leaving afterimages of their own shapes in the blurring air, the highway bending outward like a belt looped double in someone's hand, and the ocean a flat, expectant blue.

This is where your mother's accident occurred, his grandmother said.

I know, he said.

It's a shame. She should be here still.

What was she like? He had never asked this question before.

She was smart and certain of herself. Maddening. She loved your father, though what she saw in him's a mystery to me. She loved you.

What?

You were her son. Of course it changed her, having you. You changed her forever.

I wish I could remember her.

His grandmother grunted.

I said I wish, he said.

They swooped again and again to the edge of the road where it unfurled into air, and his body went limp in the seat, exhausted by the anticipation of the car taking flight, a second of thrusting ascendancy followed by a plummeting like a safe dropping through his chest. It didn't happen. Finally she cut over to the I-5, which ran down the center of the state and was less scenic and much faster, all trucks with mud flaps and bullying SUVs, all antagonistic speed. He dozed off to the straining engine and the blurring songs of radio commercials and dreamt he wasn't leaving Eureka but returning after a long absence at his mother's invitation—the fabric of the dream told him she lived in his grandmother's trailer—and was going to see her for the first time, or the first he'd remember. But he couldn't find the trailer park, though he biked along the streets he knew so well from his deliveries, streets he'd shivered down, sopping, streets that had seemed to sneer as they stretched out before him like long, riddled gutters, and then he saw the trailer being towed ahead of him by a smoke-belching truck, the back of it skidding side to side and a white scarf fluttering out a window.

He pedaled faster. Do you think you can keep going? Do you think? The voice was nervy and intimate.

I lived with her. I know what she did to you. She did it to me too, the voice said.

His handlebars twisted in one direction and the frame of the bike in the other. But you survived, the voice said. Good for you. The frame jittered as if struck by a current, and he toppled sideways. . . .

When he opened his eyes gas pumps slid into view, and the car heaved to a stop. He got out. In the convenience mart, he wandered in a daze past small bright items whose uses he knew but could not remember, until he came across a rack of potato chips. He slipped a bag of sour cream and onion under his shirt and exited to the man behind the counter calling, I can see you! The man followed him outside and right up to the car. A clear crystal on a silver chain bumped between two softish mounds that humped up from beneath the man's t-shirt. His grandmother was pumping gas.

This boy with you? the man asked.

She peered over her shoulder. What about him?

He's in the store stealing from me. I'll need you to pay for that.

He's not stealing from you.

Like hell he's not, the man said.

The boy sat in the passenger seat and freed the bag of chips and balanced it on his stomach. Scrape of nozzle being removed from the tank, clunk as it was returned to the pump.

That's the item right there, the man said.

The threads of the gas cap rasped into place. You don't understand, his grandmother said. They don't want you to. It doesn't belong to any of us.

What doesn't?

The item, as you put it. What you've come out into this day to throw your life before.

The man's face softened, grew dreamy. If it doesn't belong to us, then who does it belong to? You haven't said that. You can't say one without the other.

Oh, they keep to themselves, his grandmother said, and it seemed to the boy that they must, and that if he were one of them he would stay gone too, because if you had what you needed you could sit back and watch the others quarrel and strive, and you could pity and even love them a little as you could not if you were in the thick of it, grasping and prodding, pushing forward eagerly, naïvely, sure there was something more.

ACKNOWLEDGMENTS

Thank you Kevin Moffett, Ellis Moffett, the Vallianatos family, the MacDowell Colony, the Bread Loaf Writers' Conference, Jess Anthony, Brock Clarke, Sal Plascencia, Jason Ockert, Stefan Kiesbye, Jeff Parker, Don Morrill, Lisa Birnbaum, Alan Michael Parker, Austin Bunn, Jerry Gabriel, Karen Anderson, Stacy Elliott, Phil Zuckerman, Amy Barrett, Marcella Zita, Katherine Friedman, Rebecca Kornbluh, and Nicola Mason and Barbara Bourgoyne at Acre Books.